UNSCRUPULOUS
A Circle City Mystery

M. E. May

M&B Literary Creations

Copyright © 2015 by M. E. May
ISBN 13: 978-1519150790
ISBN 10: 1519150792

Cover Art by Julie Kukreja, Pen and Mouse Design

Edited by Mary V. Welk

Printed in the United States of America

10 9 8 7 6 5 4 3 2

DEDICATION

To my children, Brian and Marie. Although you are now adults,
there isn't anything I wouldn't do to keep you happy and safe.

OTHER NOVELS BY M. E. MAY

ACKNOWLEDGMENTS

The *Circle City Mystery Series* would be nothing without those who serve and protect the great city of Indianapolis—the men and women of the Indianapolis Metropolitan Police Department. I am especially grateful to those in the department who have been willing to answer my technical questions about the IMPD's policies and procedures.

To my faithful friends and fellow authors, Tricia Zoeller and Sue Myers for their steadfast encouragement, I give my gratitude. Without the two of you, I might have given in when I became discouraged. I also want to thank Sue, a retired nurse, for sharing her medical knowledge so I might make those portions of the novel as accurate as possible.

I wish to thank Mary V. Welk who did such a fabulous job of editing this novel. Her suggestions for changes, in addition to keeping me on the straight and narrow with grammar and punctuation, were vital to the success of this novel.

To my graphic artist, Julie Kukreja, who always creates such brilliant covers with just a few words from me, I give my deepest gratitude.

Many thanks must go to my publicist, PJ Nunn of BreakThrough Promotions for taking some of the marketing responsibilities "off my plate" and helping me reach readers across the country.

Of course, I wouldn't be able to get through all the publishing highs and lows without my family—my husband, Paul and my children, Brian and Marie. Their encouragement and support mean the world to me.

"Safety and security don't just happen, they are the result of collective consensus and public investment. We owe our children, the most vulnerable citizens in our society, a life free of violence and fear."

—Nelson Mandela, Former President of South Africa

Chapter 1

Gifts strewn across the room gave the appearance that Christmas had already come and gone. Some packages were empty while others still held their contents. Ornaments lay scattered on the floor, and some of the tree's lights had been extinguished. What had happened here?

Homicide Sergeant Brent Freeman of the Indianapolis Metropolitan Police Department shook his head as he surveyed the scene. Back in the hallway, a mother lay dead. The child in the photo on the side table was missing. What could have brought on such violence? Why take the girl?

"Ready for your first case, Detective Samuels?" he said. Anne Samuels knelt poking the debris with a pen. She'd passed the detective's exam two weeks ago and was assigned to his shift in Homicide where, as shift supervisor, he was responsible for training new detectives.

"More than ready, Sergeant. Patrol Officer Angela Sanchez was first responder."

"What did she have for us?"

Samuels stood and opened her notebook. "Officer Sanchez received a call from Dispatch at 9:12 a.m. of a deceased person at this address. She arrived at 9:24 a.m. and found the victim's mother, Elena Arroyo, outside the front door pacing and crying. Arroyo stated that when she arrived at the home, she went to the back door as she always did to find it wide open. When she entered, she cautiously approached the hallway to find her daughter lying face down in a pool of blood. She touched her daughter's arm to find her ice cold and thought she was dead. Mrs. Arroyo then searched the house, but couldn't find her granddaughter, Maricella Colon.

"Victim is Lucia Colon. She separated from her husband, Carlos, a year and a half ago. He got out of lockup about a week ago after being convicted of beating the crap out of her. Maricella is five years of age. Sanchez called Missing Persons, requesting an Amber Alert on the child."

"Why did Mrs. Colon's mother come by?"

"Elena Arroyo stopped by to take her daughter and granddaughter to the doctor's office." Samuels glanced over her shoulder towards the hallway. "I can't imagine what it would be like to find your child like this, no matter how old he or she was."

Samuels looked back at her notebook. "Elena Arroyo is waiting outside with her two sisters. Mrs. Arroyo is understandably upset, so she hasn't said much else since Sanchez arrived.

"When Sanchez entered the home, she found the victim face down in the hallway as Mrs. Arroyo had described and called it in. They'd already dispatched an ambulance, but when Sanchez checked for a pulse, she couldn't find one. She then secured the scene. Shortly after that, Patrol Officer Bays arrived to assist, followed by D. I. Spalding and the crime scene team."

"Good job, Samuels," said Brent. "I think we'll see if we can't get a little more from the mother."

Brent exited through the back of the house noticing the crooked screen door possibly damaged by the intruder. However, as he walked around to the front of the house he couldn't help but assess the older one-story home's disrepair. The wood siding could use some paint. Some of the shutters were missing, too. Obviously, Carlos wasn't Mr. Fixit.

The first winter snow had melted, and Brent could see the grass hadn't been cut for a long time. Christmas lights framed the windows on the front side of the home. Glowing brightly in the overcast morning, they added a bit of cheer to the otherwise all too depressing scene.

He found the three women standing near a large tree, probably maple from the leaves rotting on the ground. "Mrs. Arroyo?" He pulled out a pen and notebook from his coat pocket.

"Yes."

He had been correct in his assumption of which of them was the mother of the victim. A little overweight, she had a beautiful face and shoulder length silky black hair. Her sisters looked somewhat like her, but both were thinner and taller. Brent advanced toward her with dread. Talking to a loved one was hard enough. However, having to question a mother who'd just found her child brutally murdered was worse.

"Mrs. Arroyo, I'm Sergeant Freeman and this is Detective Samuels. We're from the Homicide Department. I know this is a very difficult time for you, but we'd like to ask you a few questions, if that's all right."

"Do you have children, Sergeant?" Elena asked, her voice cracking and tears streaming down her face.

Brent had heard this from grieving parents before. They never thought anyone without children could truly understand their pain, and they were correct. He simply told her no.

"Then you have no idea what this is like for me." She turned from him and paced for a few moments.

"You're right, I can only imagine how this feels. I want to find the person who did this to your daughter. I want to give her justice."

He realized he'd said the wrong thing because Mrs. Arroya stopped pacing and turned on him, her eyes burning with anger.

"Justice? You want to give my Lucia justice?" she shouted. "Like you people brought justice for my son who was shot down in the streets like a dog?"

For a moment, Brent couldn't speak. He hadn't expected to encounter someone who'd lost two of her children to violence. He watched as one of Mrs. Arroyo's sisters wrapped her arms around the distraught mother before they walked away together.

The remaining woman touched his arm. "Sergeant Freeman, I am Elena's sister Carlita Diaz. You must excuse Elena's anger. She only had Javier and Lucia. To have both of her children taken from her so brutally, and now little Maricella missing, is more than she can handle."

Brent nodded in acknowledgement. Mrs. Arroyo's situation was horrendous, but he had a job to do and couldn't waste time coddling the grieving, even if his first tendency was to do so. Having three sisters and an absent father himself, gave Brent a perspective on women's feelings most men didn't have, but he couldn't allow those feelings to cloud his judgment.

"Her son, Javier, was gunned down in the streets. He was a good boy. He made good grades and had been accepted to Purdue University's engineering program. Javier stayed away from the gangs. He was only seventeen."

"I take it when she said he didn't get justice that the shooter wasn't convicted."

"Worse. They never found out who did it," said Carlita. "There were suspicions about Los Hombres, because they'd tried to recruit him. The police stopped looking after only a couple of weeks. Elena would go in every day to ask if they'd found anything new. They finally told her not to waste her time coming in every day and said they would call her if they discovered anything new. She's never received a call, and it's been a little over two years now."

"Detective Flores just transferred over from the Gangs Unit," said Samuels.

Brent had been concentrating on his conversation with Carlita Diaz. He'd nearly forgotten about Samuels's presence.

"He might know something about the case," she continued.

"We'll talk to him when we get back to the office." Brent gave her a look he hoped would remind her to observe, not talk. He didn't want to embarrass his rookie detective on her first day. He'd have to talk to her later about jumping in with promises she may not be able to keep. Now he must direct the conversation back to this murder and apparent kidnapping.

"Ms. Diaz, do you know of anyone who might want to harm your niece and take her daughter?"

"The only person I can think of is her no-good-for-nothing husband, Carlos Colon. They were separated. He smacked her and poor little Maricella around, so she finally got brave and got a restraining order. That really ticked him off."

"Did he threaten her?" asked Brent.

"Oh, yes." Carlita nodded and took a deep breath. "He threatened to kill her all the time. They arrested Carlos arrested a year and a half ago after he nearly succeeded. He told her she didn't have any right to keep his daughter from him, like he cared about Maricella."

"What do you mean?"

"I mean, he was never around when they lived together. He went out drinking and whoring with his friends. But of course, when she'd had enough and wanted to throw him out, he started screaming about his rights."

"Thank you, Ms. Diaz. You've been a great help." Brent looked over at Elena Arroya and decided he would give her time to get over her shock. "I'll call your sister in a day or two to make an appointment to speak with her."

"Thank you, Sergeant Freeman. Of course, I can guarantee if you don't call her, she'll show up on your doorstep."

Brent smiled at her and turned to Samuels. He motioned for her to follow him to the house.

When they were a few feet away from the victim's family, Samuels stopped walking. "Sergeant, did I do something wrong back there?"

"You and I are working this case, Samuels. As much as I feel for this family, especially now that we know her son died and the case went cold, we have to be careful what we promise to do. Mrs. Arroya doesn't trust the police because of what happened to her son. It's just best to always keep to the present case."

"Okay."

"That doesn't mean we can't ask Flores about it. He may know something since he was in the gangs department when it happened."

Samuels gave him a weak smile and nodded.

"Now, let's get in there and finish looking at our crime scene."

Chapter 2

"Where is Mamá?" little Maricella whined from the back seat of the minivan. "I want to go home. I have to go to the doctor and then get ready for school."

"Cállate!" The fat woman in the front seat turned and scowled at her. "You're too young to go to school."

"Abuela Elena takes me to kindergarten…."

"I said, shut up!"

At only five, Maricella knew better than to keep talking when an angry adult started screaming at her. Her mamá always sent her to her room when Papá got mad. She would hear him yelling at Mamá and then he would break things. Sometimes he would hit Mamá and make her cry.

The fat lady finally stopped glaring at her and turned around. She was really mean. Maricella heard her hit an older boy named John right across the face before they left the big house she was taken to last night. He had a big bruise on his cheek now. The skinny man got real mad at her. He said she'd damaged the merchandise, whatever that meant. John didn't get to go with them today. He stayed at the house with a really old guy who had an ugly gray beard and never smiled.

At least the skinny man wasn't like her Papá. He got mad, but he didn't hit anybody. Last night, he came into her room in the dark and took her out of her bed. When he carried her out, she noticed her mamá sleeping on the floor in the hall in some red stuff. Maricella was confused because Mamá had never slept in the hall before.

The man put her in the back seat of a black minivan and then the fat lady brought out a paper bag and told him those were Maricella's clothes. The lady roughly put her into the seatbelt and told the man to drive. Maricella asked the man where they were going and why her mamá couldn't come.

He didn't answer, but the mean lady did. "She doesn't want you anymore, so you're going to a new home."

She couldn't understand why her mamá wouldn't want her anymore. She'd been good. Abuela Elena had told her so. Then she decided they must be taking her to her abuela's house. Even if Mamá didn't want her any longer, Abuela Elena would.

That isn't where they took her, though. The fat woman pulled her from the minivan, forcing her inside a big house in a strange neighborhood. She pushed Maricella and told her to sit on a big brown chair and not to move. Terrified, Maricella wouldn't dare move. She heard them arguing in another room. That's when she heard the woman hit John."

The fat lady said they needed to leave by five because they had to deliver Amber the next day. Maricella didn't know what time it was when she was ordered into the car, but it was still dark.

"Amber?" Maricella said to the girl in the other seat.

Amber had been looking out of the window ever since they got into the car and hadn't said a word. The girl didn't look at her; she simply continued to stare out the window.

"No talking," said the fat lady, returning to glare at her again.

Maricella lowered her eyes and nodded. She glanced momentarily at the other girl who hadn't moved, and then turned to stare out her own window at the leafless trees.

Chapter 3

Brent scanned the crime scene. "Okay, Samuels, you've been to enough crime scenes observing detectives at work. Tell me what you see."

"Our victim is lying on her stomach in the hallway of her home facing the east wall. From the blood matted in her hair, the pooling of blood around her head, and the blood spatter pattern, my first guess would be blunt force trauma. Someone struck her once with a heavy object, a person strong enough to kill her with one blow."

"How did you reach this conclusion?"

Samuels bent down and pointed. "The injury appears to be at the base of her head. If she'd been struck more than once, her injuries would be more severe. You'd also find more blood spatter in the room."

"She's pretty good," said Death Investigator Nate Spalding. "Congrats on making detective, Samuels."

Samuels stood up. "Thank you. My first guess would be that the blow snapped the spine at the base of her neck and she died before she hit the ground."

"Precisely what I think," said Spalding. "Better watch out, Freeman. She'll be replacing you before you know it."

"Whatever." Brent shook his head. "Did anyone find the weapon?"

"Not to my knowledge," said Spalding. "CSI has all the photos taken and are looking for prints and a weapon. I'm done with my preliminary. Have you seen enough? I want to transport her to the morgue."

"Yeah, go ahead." Brent turned to Samuels. "Let's go into the victim's bedroom and see if there are any clues."

They entered to find Mark Chatham, head of the CSI team, writing notes. He looked up and smiled at them.

"New partner, Freeman?"

"We switch it up in Homicide every now and then. I don't know if you've met Detective Samuels. She just joined Homicide. Anne Samuels, this is Mark Chatham, head of CSI."

She extended her hand. "I've seen you at crime scenes, but it's nice to have a formal introduction."

Chatham shook her hand. He then started flipping through his notes. "Point of entry was the back door. Not a very secure door, but it wasn't forced. I think she might have known her assailant and opened it for him."

"How did you know it was point of entry?" asked Brent.

"He left it wide open and the front door is still locked. None of the windows in the place were broken, but I printed them just in case."

Chatham pointed to the bed. "There's a novel on the bed. She was probably reading when she heard the knock on the door."

"Maybe he let himself in," said Samuels. "She had an estranged husband. He may have had a key."

Brent glanced at his partner. "Since he was in jail for beating her, I doubt it. I would think she'd have changed the locks. However, the victim's mother might know if he had, or anyone else had, a key to the place. We'll ask her once she's had a day to get over the shock."

Chatham walked toward the bedroom door and pointed down the hall. "Also, the daughter's room is a mess. Looks like someone grabbed a few of her clothes, because all the drawers are opened or pulled out and practically empty."

Brent ran his fingers through his hair as he often did when he thought things through. "Seems maybe they targeted the child, and mom became collateral damage."

"Then maybe the estranged husband isn't involved?" asked Samuels.

Brent turned to her. "Let's not rule him out yet. He may have arranged to have the child kidnapped, or may have sold her to get back at his wife for having him arrested."

Samuels's mouth dropped.

"Just because he's her parent, doesn't mean he wants her for himself. It's a control thing with this type of guy." Brent clamped his hand on Samuels' shoulder. "Everyone's a suspect until we clear them."

Samuels nodded and Brent removed his hand from her shoulder. "Anything else we should know, Chatham?"

"Not right now. We should have a preliminary report for you in a couple of days. Of course, it will take weeks for the tox and DNA stuff to come through. Lab's behind again."

"How well I know it." Brent motioned for Samuels to follow him out of the room. "We've probably seen all we can for now. We'll call and find out who's been assigned from Missing Persons and go from there. Carlos Colon is on probation, so they'll pick him up soon."

"Will we get to observe the interrogation?"

Brent smiled at her enthusiasm. "Yep, let's get back to the office and get started."

Chapter 4

Missing Persons Detective Tyrone Mayhew had requested a squad pick up Carlos Colon at the halfway house. According to Colon's parole officer, Carlos wore an ankle monitor. His parole officer said he hadn't left the house at all in the last twenty-four hours. It didn't mean he didn't have help. If he'd hired one of his buddies to take Maricella, where might they have taken her? Colon couldn't hide her at the halfway house; someone would have noticed.

Mayhew's phone rang as he studied his newly created file. "Mayhew."

"We've got your person of interest downstairs," said Patrol Officer Gavin Lloyd. "We're going to bring him up. Where do you want him?"

"Two's open. Thanks, Lloyd. I'll see you in a few."

Mayhew hung up the phone, closed the file, and then got up and walked towards the interrogation rooms. Before he reached the hallway, he saw Sergeant Freeman and Detective Samuels coming off the elevator.

"Heard you got the Maricella Colon case," said Freeman.

"That's right." Tyrone switched his attention to Samuels. "Congrats on making detective."

"Thanks." Samuels smiled, blushing slightly.

Officer Lloyd came towards them. "He's ready for you,

Detective."

"Thanks, Lloyd." Mayhew turned to Freeman. "I've got the murder victim's husband in two. You want to observe?"

"Yes, we would," said Samuels, brightening before turning a deeper shade of red.

"Don't be embarrassed at your own enthusiasm," said Mayhew. "Enjoy it while you can. Come on, you two. Time to watch the master at work."

He watched as Freeman and Samuels entered the observation room and then unlocked the door to Interrogation Room Two. There sat a muscular Hispanic man Mayhew guessed would be about six-two if he stood up. His neck was so heavily tattooed; Mayhew thought there must be a real art show under his coat.

"Mr. Colon, I'm Detective Mayhew of the Missing Persons Department."

"Yeah," Colon said, leaning forward. His piercing deep brown eyes glared menacingly. "If somebody's missin', I ain't got nothin' to do with it."

"Did the officers tell you anything about why we asked you to come down here?"

"I didn't exactly *come down*, now did I? They drug me out of the halfway house. Didn't seem like I had much choice."

"Well, this is pretty serious and personal, Mr. Colon. We didn't think you'd want to discuss it in front of your fellow parolees."

"Serious and personal, huh? Just give it up already. I got things to do. Sittin' around here all day isn't one of them."

"When did you see you wife, Lucia Colon, last?"

"She sayin' I did somethin'? She just wants to put me back in jail. I only been out for two weeks and I ain't seen her or my daughter in over a year."

"Your parole officer says you didn't go anywhere after your shift at the grocery store yesterday."

"That's right." Colon slammed back in his chair and crossed his arms over his chest.

"You watch the news today?"

"I don't watch the news. It's too depressin'."

Colon smirked at Mayhew in the macho in control way men who have no real confidence or control do. Tyrone wanted to hit him, but refrained, tightening his jaw and smiling instead.

"Well, then you don't know somebody murdered your wife sometime last night."

That wiped the smirk off Colon's face. Slowly sitting up, his mouth agape, he put his arms on the table while avoiding eye contact with Mayhew. His face paled, and his eyes shifted from side to side. Unless Colon had become a great actor, his reaction showed him to be a man who didn't expect to hear this news.

"So, I take it this is all news to you."

Colon slowly looked up at Mayhew, his face regaining more than its normal color. He now looked furious. "You tellin' me somebody killed my Lucia?"

Mayhew thought the man's head would burst, or steam would come rolling out of his ears at any moment. "Now you see why I didn't want anybody talking to you at the halfway house? This is too personal."

Slamming his fists on the table, Colon let out a noise that sounded like an enraged dog growling. He stood up and paced angrily.

"Mr. Colon, I know this is hard, but you need to stay calm and sit back down," said Mayhew as he stood up in a defensive stance.

"How do you expect me to stay calm? You tell me my wife is

dead and somebody murdered her, and you want me to calm down?"

"That's right, because I have something else to tell you."

Comprehension suddenly put something like fear on Colon's face. He sat down in his chair and stared at Mayhew. "Where's my daughter?"

"Maricella is missing. That's why I'm involved. We think someone kidnapped her."

"You think someone….are you sure she's not with Lucia's mother?"

"Mrs. Arroyo called us when she found her daughter's body. Somebody grabbed a handful of Maricella's clothes and took her. Our homicide detectives think she was the target all along and your wife died trying to stop whoever did this."

Colon slumped forward, his elbows resting on his knees and his head in his hands. The range of this man's emotions surprised Tyrone. The only thing the man hadn't done was cry.

"Mr. Colon, do you have any idea who might have wanted to take your daughter?"

"No." He shook his head more times than necessary.

"Did you have someone take her to get back at your wife?"

"NO! I loved Lucia. I would never hurt her."

"Really? What were you in jail for…oh yeah. I believe you were convicted of beating the crap out of your wife."

Colon sat back in his chair again, his face turned away from Mayhew.

"'Course, you send somebody over there to do your dirty work, maybe they go too far. Lucia wasn't supposed to be killed, maybe just roughed up a little. Guy got a little carried away or didn't want to leave a witness."

"I didn't have anything to do with this. Now what are you doing to find Maricella?"

Mayhew recognized the intent glare of a half frightened-half angry father. Something he'd felt when his own son was shot last summer.

"An Amber Alert has been issued. People get all worked up and are good about calling in when they see a child's been abducted. In the meantime, we need to look at people who were close to her. Someone the family knows usually commits child abductions, and it appears Lucia let her attacker in. Neither you nor Maricella's grandmother could give us an idea of who took her—unless you're holding back on me."

"I'm not," Colon spat. "I don't have any idea who would want to take Maricella."

"You have any enemies who might do this to get back at *you*? Make anybody mad while you were in prison?"

"I wasn't in with no hard core bunch. They don't bother when you only got nine months. I didn't talk about my kid in there. It was none of their business."

"Okay, what about people on the outside? A guy like you who enjoys beatin' up women could have an old girlfriend or two who might want to get back at him."

Colon wrinkled his brow and then turned his eyes to Mayhew. "Yeah. Isabella Peña."

"How long ago did you date her?"

"Two, three years ago."

"So you cheated on your wife."

"I'm a man. I got needs. Lucia was too tired all the time."

"Or maybe too beat up?"

Colon shook his head and then continued. "Isabella was always tellin' me she'd have her brother, Alberto, bash my head in if I hit her. She had a real mouth on her."

"Do you think she—or her brother—is capable of kidnapping and murdering someone just to get back at you?"

"I don't think so, but who knows. People are always turning out to be different than you think they are."

"Okay, Mr. Colon. You sit tight and I'll get a patrol officer to take you back to the halfway house. We'll let you know if we need to talk to you again."

"Just find my Maricella. Don't let nothing happen to her."

"I got four kids of my own. You better believe I'm going to do everything humanly possible to find her."

Mayhew unlocked the door and entered the hallway. As he pulled the door shut, he paused and thought about his family—those three rambunctious boys and his sweet little baby girl. He would be devastated if this happened to one of his children.

He heard the door open to his right. Samuels and Freeman emerged from the observation room. "Come on over to my desk, you two. We need to talk."

Chapter 5

"I'd bet my next paycheck he's not your guy," said Mayhew. "Guys like him don't lose track and stop talking. This guy genuinely showed surprise when I told him about the murder."

"He's obviously upset about his daughter's disappearance as well." Brent ran his fingers through his golden brown locks. "It looks like we need to find out more about the Peña siblings."

"That's what I'd do," said Mayhew. "What do you think, Detective Samuels?"

"I agree."

"We need to get to our desks and write up what we have so far," said Brent. "I also want to talk to Detective Flores about looking into a cold case. Mrs. Arroyo told us her son Javier was killed in a drive by a few years back. Maybe Flores heard something when he worked in Gangs."

"Good luck, my friends." Mayhew reached out and shook each of their hands in turn. "Keep me up-to-date. You never know when one of us will come up with a suspect and could solve both cases."

"You've got it. Let's go, Samuels."

Brent arrived in the Homicide Department with Samuels trailing behind him. He found Major Robert Stevenson talking to Detective Tomas Flores.

"Major," said Brent as he approached the pair.

Stevenson acknowledged him with a nod. "Flores, Sergeant Freeman is day shift supervisor. You'll check in with him for your assignments. Welcome to the department." He then turned and walked back to his office.

"Ready to get your feet wet?" asked Brent.

Flores nodded.

"By the way, this is Detective Anne Samuels. She just moved up from patrol. We're working on a case involving a Hispanic female victim killed in her home on the west side sometime in the last twelve hours. Her daughter is missing and it looks like a child abduction."

"The Amber Alert go out?" asked Flores.

"As soon as we realized she was missing. Detective Tyrone Mayhew from Missing Persons is helping us on that end. He's already interviewed the father. At this point, it appears he's not involved, but we haven't ruled him out."

"Anything I can do to help?"

"Funny you should ask." Brent smiled and motioned for Flores to accompany him to his desk. He sat down at the computer and brought up the Javier Arroyo cold case.

"Our victim, Lucia Colon, had a brother, Javier Arroyo. Their mother discovered Lucia's body this morning."

"Did I hear you say *had?*" asked Flores.

"You heard him right," said Samuels, speaking for the first time. "The mother, Elena Arroyo, was pretty hostile towards us. She doesn't feel we did enough to find her son's killer, and now she has to face this."

"I don't remember that case. Are you thinking about reinvestigating?" asked Flores. "Did the mother have anyone in mind for either incident?"

"She didn't want to speak with us at the scene, so we talked to the victim's aunt who told us about Javier. I do think we should take a quick look at it." Brent sat down, offering Flores the side chair. "Samuels, start looking up the Peña siblings. We need to check them out as soon as possible."

"So what do you want from me?" asked Flores.

"I want you to check into the Javier Arroyo case. It never hurts to look at it again, especially since you didn't work on it the first time. Fresh eyes might uncover something new."

"Okay. Did this aunt think the cases were related?"

"No, she couldn't think of anyone who would harm her niece, except maybe the estranged husband, Carlos Colon. Samuels and I watched Mayhew's interrogation of Colon. The guy's a piece of work, but way too upset about Lucia and freaking out about his kid. He also has an alibi. He's got an ankle bracelet and his PO told us he was at the halfway house the whole night."

Flores nodded. "I've heard of Carlos. He's with Los Hombres, so if he lost it in there, he's serious. He never loses his cool with the cops."

"According to the aunt, they think the son's murder was gang related, but Javier wasn't in a gang. The aunt thinks they may have been pressuring him to join. When he didn't, they shot him."

"I'll ask around, but I can tell you, if it's gang related and they haven't pinned it on anyone yet, they probably never will," said Flores.

"I feel for Mrs. Arroyo. She's lost both of her children to violence, and now her granddaughter is missing. We won't spend a lot of time on the Arroyo murder, but I'd like for you to pull the cold case file and evidence. Go over it and let me know if there's anything we should check. Hopefully, between you, Samuels, Mayhew, and I, we can find some sort of closure for this family."

"You've got it, Sergeant," said Flores.

"Hey, Sarge," said Erica Barnes.

He waved her over. "Detective Erica Barnes, this is Tomas Flores. He's our newest day shift detective. I'd like for you to show him around the department before he goes down to the evidence locker."

"Can't the guy even get a cup of coffee before you put him to work?"

Brent gave her his best "can it Barnes" look and she threw up her hands.

Barnes extended her hand. "Welcome to Homicide, Flores, where all of your super cop dreams come true."

Brent watched as she left with Flores. One of these days, he'd have to find a way to repay her. His desk phone rang.

"Sergeant Freeman, there's an Elena Arroyo here to see you."

"Good. Have her brought up to the conference room."

"Will do."

"Samuels, Mrs. Arroyo is here. I'm going to put you in charge of the questioning because I think she'll relate to a woman more easily. You up for it?"

Samuels eyes widened and she smiled broadly. "Yes, sir. I believe I can handle it."

Brent stood up and grabbed his notebook. He enjoyed her enthusiasm, but he had to say one more thing. "Samuels, please don't call me sir. If Barnes hears you call me sir, she'll make my life miserable."

Chapter 6

Anne could see the tension in Elena Arroyo's body language. The rigid set of her jaw, the anger radiating from her eyes, and the tightly crossed arms spanning her chest combined to melt away Anne's excitement for the opportunity Sergeant Freeman had given her. Mrs. Arroyo's attitude caused Anne's heart to beat much too quickly. She hoped she wouldn't break out into a sweat, or worse, start blushing.

A quick glance from her supervisor gave her the go ahead to take over. Anne sat down next to Mrs. Arroyo while Freeman took the seat across from them.

"Hello, Mrs. Arroyo. I'm Detective Samuels. I'm so sorry for your loss."

"Really, Detective? You feel bad that another one of us is dead? You gonna tell me now how hard you're gonna work to find who killed my daughter? You know, like how hard you all worked at finding who killed my son."

"Mrs. Arroyo, I have two sons, and I don't know what I would do if anything happened to them." Samuels looked intently into Mrs. Arroyo's dark brown eyes and saw them soften slightly. "When you told Sergeant Freeman about your son this morning, he looked into it. He's having one of our detectives go over the old evidence and interviews done at the time of the murder. This detective is new to the case, so we're hoping he'll find something the investigating officer missed the first time around."

Anne paused and Mrs. Arroyo let her arms relax, uncrossing them. She looked away from Anne, momentarily glancing around the room. Mrs. Arroyo then fixed her gaze on Freeman.

"Thank you." Mrs. Arroyo no longer clenched her jaw, but she didn't smile either. No one would under these circumstances.

With Mrs. Arroyo more receptive, Anne began her inquiry. "We know this is difficult, but we need to know if there is anyone you feel could have done this. Did your daughter have any enemies?"

"On the day he was sentenced, that good for nothing husband of hers said he would kill her next time he saw her."

"Carlos Colon has a solid alibi," said Anne. "He seems to think an ex-girlfriend might have had something to do with it."

Mrs. Arroyo rolled her eyes. "If you're talking about Isabella Peña, you're wrong. That girl felt sorry for my Lucia. She knew how it felt to be with Carlos."

Anne nodded at the logic of her statement. "Carlos told Detective Mayhew that Isabella's brother, Alberto, hated him and might have hurt Lucia and taken his daughter to get back at him."

"No. No. Alberto wouldn't hurt Lucia and take Maricella. He hated Carlos for how he hurt Isabella. He knew how my Lucia was being treated. If he wanted to kill someone, he would have gone after Carlos."

"We'll probably talk to them anyway. They may know something that could be helpful." Anne pushed a loose strand of hair behind her ear. "So is Carlos the only person you feel had reason to commit these two crimes?"

"No." Mrs. Arroyo leaned forward. "Los Hombres. I've always believed they were responsible for killing my son. I've been telling people that for a long time, so maybe this is how they get back at me."

"Did you suspect any one person in particular of killing your son?"

"I always suspected Hector Fuentes."

"Why do you think Fuentes was involved?" asked Freeman.

"Hector was the leader," said Mrs. Arroyo, a scowl forming on her face. "He wanted Javier to join the gang and my son refused. You don't tell Hector Fuentes no. Javier was a good boy. He never missed school. He didn't hang around with a bad crowd. My son wanted to be an engineer. He wanted to do something with his life. But…." Mrs. Arroyo's eyes filled with tears.

"Fuentes went to prison over a year ago, convicted of first degree murder. He'd been awaiting trial two years prior to that," said Freeman.

"Ah, yes. I know this. But do not think for even a moment Hector doesn't still run things in the neighborhood."

Freeman gave Anne a slight nod. It seemed to be time to conclude for now. "Mrs. Arroyo, you've been very helpful. We will make sure Detective Mayhew gets your contact information since he is assigned to your granddaughter's case. Of course, you may also hear from Detective Flores in a few days regarding your son's case."

Mrs. Arroyo nodded wearily. Anne wanted to pull her up into a hug and tell her everything would be all right, but she refrained. She had a hard time keeping a professional demeanor while watching people in such horrendous pain.

Freeman called for an officer to escort Mrs. Arroyo downstairs and motioned for Anne to follow him back to their desks.

"Great interview, Samuels. Now, what would you do next?"

"I think we should ask Detective Mayhew to interview the Peña siblings while we have a talk with Hector Fuentes."

"My thoughts precisely. It looks like we'll be going to

Michigan City first thing tomorrow."

Chapter 7

It had been a long day. Brent wanted nothing more than to grab a beer and sit in front of the television while holding his beautiful Natalie in his arms. He'd met Natalie when he testified in the trial that finally put Hector Fuentes away. From the moment her beautiful crystal blue eyes met his, she had him hooked.

Brent put his key in the door, but it flew open before he could unlock it.

"Surprise!"

Brent stepped back, astonished to see his twin sister smiling at him. Brenda threw her arms around him and hugged him tightly. Peering over her shoulder, he could see Natalie grinning and shrugging, apparently also caught unaware of their guest's plan to visit.

"Sis, what are you doing in Indy?"

"Veterinarian convention." She stood back and put her hands on his arms, looking him over. "I didn't call because I wanted to surprise you."

"It worked." He hoped Natalie wasn't upset by it because this probably wouldn't be the last time one of his sisters would pull this on them.

Brenda stepped aside so he could come in out of the cold. Then she pulled the keys from the door, jingling them at him. "Some policeman you are."

He turned and she tossed the keys to him. "Believe it or not, I'm human." Then he glanced over at Natalie.

"I asked your sister if she had a favorite restaurant so we can treat her to dinner."

There went Brent's dream of a quiet, restful evening. "I'm guessing Mexican."

"You bet, bro." Brenda punched his arm and grabbed her coat off the back of the couch. "Tijuana Flats is okay with me. You two ready to go? I'm starving."

Brent saw Natalie's tense smile. A creature of habit and someone who planned everything, she had a hard time dealing with change. He hoped she'd adjust. Otherwise, how would she fit in with his crazy family?

Only ten minutes away, they arrived at the restaurant, ordered their food, and were served in record time. This was the first place he'd taken Mandy Stevenson when they were dating. It seemed like so long ago and yet like it had been yesterday. Even if Mandy hadn't decided marrying a cop wasn't in her life plans, the relationship would have been difficult with her father as his boss.

Brenda shut her eyes in a dreamy, satisfied manner. "Nobody does enchiladas like the Flats. How's your burrito?"

Brent had just taken a mouthful of food. He had a feeling Brenda had purposely waited until that precise moment to ask her question. All three of his sisters had picked on him relentlessly growing up, but Brenda usually less than the older two. They were twins after all. They'd shared a womb for eight and a half months and had a special bond not felt with the others.

Brent chewed and swallowed before speaking. He wasn't going to give her the satisfaction of seeing him talk with his mouth full. "Delicious. So how long are you going to be in town?"

"I'll be here through the weekend. The convention is only three days, but I want to do some shopping while I'm here. Mom's birthday is next week, you know."

"I'm very well aware."

"Natalie, you'll find Brent is very good at remembering special occasions. He never forgets birthdays, anniversaries, et cetera."

"Yes, your brother is very considerate."

Brent had a hard time swallowing his next bite of burrito as he felt Natalie's comment was a jab at Brenda's unexpected visit. Of course, his sister hadn't seemed to take it that way as she plunged into her next round of conversation.

"I'm staying at the Hyatt downtown. If you have some time, maybe we could go shopping on Sunday. Natalie, you should come along. You need to get to know the family traditions if you plan on keeping him."

"Sounds like fun." Natalie seemed to relax now that she knew they weren't going to have a house guest...that and/or the two margaritas she'd consumed.

"So....since you two spent Thanksgiving with Natalie's parents...Mom wanted to know if you'd spend Christmas with us."

Brent hadn't really discussed this with Natalie yet. He'd hoped she would agree, but wanted the chance to ask her himself. He tensed, angry Brenda would put them on the spot like this.

Fortunately, Natalie took him off the proverbial hook. "Of course, we'd love to come. Mom and Dad will be leaving next week for their condo in Fort Myers. I'm hoping to talk your brother into taking some time off this winter so we can go visit them."

"Well, that's settled. Our mother is *so* into Christmas. I don't know what Brent's told you about our father, but I think Mom always overdid Christmas to make up for all the misery Dad inflicted."

Brent couldn't help but let his mind wander to little Maricella.

His father was almost as bad as hers. The abuse his father inflicted through his drinking wasn't physical, but psychological and financial in nature. At least he had his mother and sisters. Maricella must be so frightened right now.

"Earth to Brent," said his sister as she waved her hands in front of his face. "Where were you just now?"

"Just thinking about a new case I'm on."

Natalie glanced at him with sympathetic eyes. Her office had probably caught wind of the murder and kidnapping by now.

"I can't say much about it except someone murdered a woman and took her little girl. We talked to the husband today, but we're pretty sure he had nothing to do with it. The victim's mother is really shaken up. Her son was killed a couple of years ago."

"Oh, no," said Brenda. "It must be even harder to have something like this happen during the holidays. There's an Amber Alert out, right?"

"The second we realized she was missing. Tyrone Mayhew is lead on her case."

Natalie smiled. "He's a good man and a great detective. I'm sure he'll find her."

Brent looked down at the rest of his food. He'd lost his appetite. This little girl could be out of state by now. If a family member hadn't taken her, then who did? What would they want with a five-year-old? He didn't want to think about the possibilities.

"Well, I'm stuffed and ready to get settled into my hotel room." Brenda put her hand on Brent's shoulder. "You're a great detective. You'll figure this out, I'm sure of it. Now let's get back to your place so I can get my car."

Brent nodded, no longer resentful of her surprise visit. It was always good to see his twin and to remember where he came from.

It helped him to empathize with others in a job that often left a person jaded.

He helped Natalie shrug into her coat. Without further conversation, they left the restaurant, got into his car, and headed home.

Chapter 8

Maricella pulled the covers up over her head. It was very cold in this place. When she'd asked the mean lady, Nina, where they were, she sent her to bed without any supper. Her arm ached where Nina had grabbed it to shake her. It hurt really bad. For a moment, Maricella thought her arm would be ripped off, just like the time when her Papá ripped off her doll's arm. Course, dollies couldn't feel stuff.

Her tummy hurt. She'd only had a peanut butter sandwich and some water for lunch. She didn't mean to be bad.

Lots of noises were coming from the other room, making it too hard to fall asleep. In addition to the girl who'd sat beside her in the car, she'd seen two bigger children in the house, another girl and a boy. Nobody told her their names because she got sent to bed. The first girl she'd met was right. She'd better not talk unless Nina asked her a question. This was too hard.

She missed her mamá. Her mamá would never give her away. Not when Mamá would get so upset if she couldn't see Maricella when she played outside. And her abuela would never let Mamá give her away, not to mean people.

Did they miss her? Did Papá know about this? He could be really mean too, but he said he loved her.

Her thoughts were interrupted when she heard the doorknob turning. Burrowing deeper under the covers, she waited. Maybe if they thought she was sleeping, they'd leave her alone.

The door opened and shut quietly. Soft footsteps approached her. Maricella could tell this person was being sneaky. Then she felt a light touch on her back and couldn't help but jerk.

"Don't be scared, little girl."

The unfamiliar voice came in a whisper. A boy's voice. It had to be the boy she saw when she arrived. She lay very still; afraid of what he might do to her.

"It's okay. I know you're awake. I can't stay long. I told them I was going to the bathroom."

He gently pulled at the covers and she trembled at this stranger's silhouette. Being all alone, she couldn't scream because nobody would help her. However, he didn't try to grab her or even sit on her bed, so she started to relax a little. It was hard to see him in the faint light of the moon, but she could see he was tall and thin.

"My name is Jack. What's yours?"

At first, her throat was so tight she could only squeak out her name.

"What?" he asked.

Swallowing hard, she cleared her throat and tried again. "Maricella."

"That's a really pretty name." Jack reached into his pocket and pulled out a smashed roll. "I snuck this for you. I couldn't bring any water, so pinch off small bites, okay?"

Maricella nodded.

"Eat it under the covers so no one sees it."

"Jack!" the mean lady screamed.

"I got to get back. I'll see you in the morning." He turned away and walked to the door. As he left the room, he called out, "I'm coming!"

Maricella looked at the roll then sniffed it. She took a little bite as Jack had instructed. Except for being flattened and covered with a piece or two of lint, it tasted sweet and made her belly feel better. She pulled the blanket back over her head, continuing to eat a tiny pinch at a time.

It appeared not everyone else here was hateful. Jack would look out for her.

Chapter 9

Instead of taking Samuels to Michigan City, Brent decided to assign Detectives Tomas Flores and Chennelle Kendall to interview Hector Fuentes at the prison. Considering his recent history with Fuentes, he'd decided sending someone else to speak with him was best for their cases. Even if they didn't get anything new on the Javier Arroyo case, maybe they could get a hint as to who had killed his sister and taken his niece.

This wasn't the only reason Brent decided not to go. Natalie hadn't reacted well to the fact Brent and Anne Samuels would be going upstate together. Her attitude confused him. Erica Barnes had been his partner for several years, and Natalie seemed okay about her. Then again, Erica was living with Ben Jacobs while Anne was getting a divorce. In her job as a prosecutor, Natalie appeared to have unwavering confidence, but in their relationship, it seemed to melt away.

The Peña interviews were essential. He assigned Detective Samuels to accompany Detective Mayhew on his interrogation of Alberto Peña. Brent would go alone to speak with Isabella.

Isabella worked at a hair salon on the far west side called Le Femme. She had told Brent on the phone she had some time between haircuts at 9:00 a.m., so he agreed to meet her there rather than having her come to the station.

He pulled into the little strip mall off of West Washington Street and found the salon easily. The sign on the building just above the door showed the name of the establishment painted in a

34

bright medicinal pink. He entered the salon to the strong smells of curling solutions, dyes and hairspray.

"May I help you?" asked the very young, purple haired receptionist sitting at the front desk. She wore two giant nose rings and Brent found it almost impossible not to stare at them.

"I'm here to speak with Isabella Peña."

"Okay. She's in the back. You wait right over there and I'll get her."

When she stood, Brent saw she wore a very tight, short, black leather skirt with fishnet hose and short boots with four-inch heels. He puzzled over how she walked in them without falling, and how she'd kept warm in that outfit.

Brent took a seat in the waiting area and looked around. A woman dressed all in black with black spiky hair sat in one of the chairs—probably a stylist waiting for her next appointment to arrive. Across from her, a blonde male in sensible shoes, jeans, and a tight black tee shirt set a gray-haired woman's rather short hair in small curlers. They were chatting away about Christmas shopping and how expensive everything was nowadays.

From the corner of his eye, Brent saw a tall woman with long, silky dark hair coming toward him from the back of the salon. Her jeans fit snugly on a much too skinny frame, and she wore a burgundy sweater. The receptionist trailing behind her smiled at Brent before taking her seat at the desk.

If Natalie could see him surrounded by all of these tight jeaned, mini skirted women, would she have chosen for him to take the road trip with Samuels instead?

"I assume you are Detective Freeman," Isabella said, her voice deep and sensuous. "You said you wanted to ask me some questions about Carlos Colon. I heard someone killed his wife, and his daughter is missing. He was a cruel man, so it wouldn't surprise me if he is the one who did this."

"Actually, we spoke with Mr. Colon. He has a solid alibi. He seems genuinely upset about his missing daughter."

Isabella raised her eyebrows. "Really? Carlos never struck me as father of the year. How do you know he isn't putting on an act?"

"You knew him. Do you honestly think he can act that well?"

"Probably. He fooled many women with his charms before he started smacking them around."

"I see your point," said Brent.

Isabella crossed her arms. "So if you didn't come to ask me if I think he did it, why are you here?"

"Because you and your brother, Alberto, are the only names *he* could come up with who might hate him enough to commit these crimes."

Isabella threw back her head in hysterical laughter. "You must be joking. Oh, this is just like Carlos. Detective Freeman, if my brother or I wanted to get back at Carlos, we wouldn't harm his wife or child. They suffered enough at his hands. I would have had someone beat Carlos until he couldn't move, and then I would have kicked him like the dog he is. I hated the man, not his family."

"Do you have any idea who might have wanted to harm Lucia Colon?"

"No. After I ended the affair, I went to visit her to apologize. I even tried to help her get away from him, but she was too scared. After he put her into the hospital the last time, Alberto and I went to see her there. That's when we met her mother. Between the three of us, we convinced Lucia to prosecute Carlos. Believe me; we were all very disappointed he only got nine months."

"Thank you for your time, Ms. Peña. Let us know if you think of anything else or if you hear anything suspicious."

Isabella nodded and left with an exaggerated sway in her boney hips. Brent thought she might be anorexic. He left the salon and got into his, car anxious to find out how Mayhew and Samuels' interview went with Alberto.

Chapter 10

Brent arrived just in time to find Samuels and Mayhew escorting a young Hispanic man from the interrogation area. Samuels nodded at him as she entered the elevator with her suspect.

"Hey, Brent," said Mayhew. "How'd it go with the sister?"

"Another dead end. She immediately accused Carlos Colon."

"Same here. He's got an alibi we're gonna check on, but he says if he wanted to get back at Carlos for what he'd done to Isabella, he would have killed him, not Lucia. Matter of fact, he and the sister are the ones who convinced Lucia to press charges the last time Carlos beat her."

"I got the same story from the sister. When we talked to Elena Arroyo yesterday, she was adamant the Peñas couldn't have done this."

"Guys." Brent turned at the familiar voice of Sergeant Ben Jacobs, who often partnered with Mayhew. "I've got something here the lieutenant thought you should see."

He handed the folders to Mayhew. "Those are cases of missing children who were abducted from their homes recently. Amber Neal is nine, Caucasian with dark hair and eyes. She was last seen on November third by the babysitter who tucked her into bed. The sitter fell asleep on the couch with her headset on. She woke up when the parents came in, and just as the father started to leave to take her home, Mom starts screaming. Amber's bedroom was in disarray, clothes taken and the girl gone.

"Tamia Franks, age ten, went out on Halloween with friends to trick or treat. Her friends said they went up to a house, but when they turned to see why Tamia hadn't come up to the door, she had vanished."

"What about the boy?" asked Mayhew, glancing at the other file.

"John Balor, age eight, blond hair and blue eyes. He vanished on October fifteenth in the middle of the night sometime after the parents went to sleep. They got in through the kid's window. It had been a warm day. He apparently didn't lock the window when he closed it. Same thing—missing kid, missing clothes."

Brent combed his hair with his hand. "At age eight, you'd think the boy would have tried to fight off his kidnappers."

Mayhew shook his head. "Not if the perpetrator threatened to kill his parents if he didn't cooperate. They move these kids pretty fast. Some of the older ones may have been sold already. They may not even be in the U. S."

Brent nodded. "So, the only real difference is the parents and babysitter weren't killed in any of these cases."

"Precisely," said Jacobs. "The lieutenant thought these were much too similar to be a coincidence."

"I agree," said Mayhew. "I'm gonna go back to my desk and do a search further back. See if there are any others. We may be looking at something much more sinister than payback here."

Brent knew exactly what this could mean—human trafficking.

Chapter 11

Detectives Flores and Kendall arrived at the Indiana State Prison facility at 10:00 a.m. After signing in and surrendering everything in their possession, a guard escorted them to a visitation room. The superintendant had been very cooperative in allowing them to question Hector Fuentes on such short notice and had assured them their session would be recorded.

"You meet Fuentes when you worked gangs?" asked Kendall.

"No, but I met some of his *friends*. The department wanted to take Fuentes down in the worst way, but his isn't the only gang in Indy. I'd been working with Chuck Neelan on a Russian gang before I got word my transfer went through."

"I heard those guys are ruthless."

"Them and the gangs coming up from South America. It's worse in Chicago. I forget how many gangs they have now. Hundreds."

"Why so many?" asked Kendall.

"Because everybody wants everything right now. Gang members used to start at the bottom and work their way up. Now, if a member has ambitions, he just breaks away and creates his own gang. It makes it really tough to keep track."

"I can imagine. Glad you're with us now. We've been short-handed for a while."

"Thanks, I—." Tomas didn't have a chance to finish his sentence. The door swung open and the prisoner walked in, manacled at his ankles and wrists.

The guard pointed at the chains. "You want these removed?"

Tomas shook his head and the guard shoved Fuentes into a chair.

Fuentes's bald head gleamed in the fluorescent light, and his wide grin spoke of his intention to provoke and sidestep any questions. Tomas had seen this before. The arrogance, the need to be in control. He'd also seen more than one cop lose it during interrogation, but that wouldn't be happening today. Not on his part anyway.

"Mr. Fuentes, I'm Detective Kendall and this is—"

"I know who he is." Fuentes leaned forward glaring at Tomas. "He chose to deny his blood. Instead of joining us, he chose to fight us."

"We all make choices others don't like," said Kendall. "Detective Flores is now in the Homicide Department and we came today to ask you a few questions about an old homicide."

"If you want me to give up my own, you wasted a trip, chica."

Fuentes's lip curled as he sat back in his chair. The look he gave Detective Kendall had more venom in it than the one he'd given Tomas. Then she remembered Fuentes had killed a member of an African American gang for dating his sister. He hated people of Chennelle's race.

"How about some respect, Hector," said Tomas.

"Whatever."

Tomas decided he'd better take the lead in questioning. His partner gave a slight nod indicating she knew what needed to be done. He decided to use Fuentes's first name to make it more personal.

"Hector, do you remember Javier Arroyo?"

"Yeah, I remember him."

"Rumor has it you're the one who shot him."

Tomas sat back now waiting for the silence to break. He wanted to see Hector's reaction. As usual, Hector sneered and looked at Tomas with no need to show emotion. Emotion is what put him in here. Up to then, he'd been on the streets for twenty years without being caught.

"Is this the way it's going to be?" asked Tomas. "You see, we've got a big problem. Somebody murdered Javier's sister, Lucia Colon, and kidnapped her five-year-old daughter."

"Why is that my concern?" asked Fuentes.

"Hector, we all know it doesn't matter you're in here. You still get messages to your boys and they carry out your orders. We also heard a rumor Lucia's husband, Carlos Colon, had ticked you off. Is that true?"

"Let me put it to you this way," Fuentes said, leaning forward again. "Carlos hurts women and kids, not me. Nobody from Los Hombres would hurt a kid. Nobody."

"You're sure about that."

Fuentes glanced up at the small one-by-one foot window near the ceiling. Tomas waited again in silence, almost forgetting about Detective Kendall.

"Okay, Fuentes, enough of this crap!" Kendall got out of her chair with fire in her eyes. She leaned on the table, almost nose to nose with Fuentes. "I don't care about your gang stuff. All I care about is that little girl. Did you kill Javier Arroyo? Did you have his sister killed to get back at his mother for nagging the police? Did you have them kidnap Maricella to make her father pay for hurting your little feelings?"

"Get out of my face!" He spat in her face.

Tomas jumped up from his seat, but Chennelle stood her ground, glaring into Fuentes's eyes as the glob ran down her cheek. Then she spoke in a low menacing growl. "We need to find Maricella Colon. Do you have any idea what is going on out there? You said you and your buddies don't hurt children. If that's true, then why not help us find her?"

"This one has some huevos." Fuentes squinted at her and then sat back in his chair.

Chennelle sat back in her chair as well and pulled a napkin from her pocket. Tomas wondered if she'd experienced something like this before. He could learn a lot from this one.

"I'm gonna tell you what I been tellin' the cops for years now. I didn't have anything to do with Javier Arroyo. We asked him to join us, and some of the guys might have been putting on some pressure, but nobody in Los Hombres put him down."

Tomas nodded. "Any idea who did it?"

"Yeah, I do. We take care of our own."

Tomas could feel his face heating up. Fuentes had known all along who killed Javier and said nothing. "If it's taken care of, you can tell us. Then his mother can be at peace knowing his killer got what he deserved."

Fuentes rocked slightly, pursing his lips. He looked from side to side then leaned forward, his forearms on his thighs. "Elena Arroyo is one stubborn woman. Now she lost both her children. I guess she deserves some peace, but I'm not giving up my man. Just tell her a member of the Blood Brothers killed Javier. Go back to your office and look up murders two weeks after Arroyo bought it and you'll find your killer."

"Another unsolved?" asked Tomas.

Hector Fuentes shrugged and said no more.

Chapter 12

"I told you to clean up this mess!" Nina, the mean lady who brought her here, slapped the boy named Jack across the back of his head. "What are you staring at? You want some, too?"

Maricella cowered and turned away, waiting for the blow. It didn't happen. She heard Nina's heavy steps as she left them in the kitchen. Slowly, she turned to Jack.

"I'm okay," he whispered. "She doesn't hit very hard; I can take it. Just try not to make her mad. You're a lot smaller than me, so it might hurt you more."

She nodded, not knowing what to say. Maricella still couldn't understand why her mamá would send her to live in this terrible place. She never had to sweep and scrub floors at home. Mamá made her bed, fixed her stuff to eat, and protected her from Papá. Why would she send her to a place where no one would protect her—except maybe Jack.

Jack had been washing dishes while she swept the floor. The broom was taller than she and hard to control. When the broom handle hit a jar on the counter, it fell to the floor and broke. Jack had taken the blame. Yelling angrily, Nina had jerked him hard and pushed him to the floor.

Now Maricella could see Jack's hand bleeding from falling on a jagged piece of glass. Despite his wound, he took her dustpan and used it to scoop up the broken bits. She approached him and asked quietly, "Do you need the broom?"

"I'll pick up the big pieces first," he said. "Then we can sweep up the little pieces. You okay?"

Maricella blushed. She felt bad Nina had hurt him. It seemed funny for him to ask her if she was okay. "Yes, but why did you tell her you did it?"

"Like I said, I can take it. I don't like it when she picks on the little kids. She should have given you a different job, like folding laundry or washing dishes. Sweeping should be done by somebody taller."

"I never had to do stuff like this when I lived at home. Abuela Elena never had me do housework either."

"What's Abuela?"

"Grandmother."

"So, can you speak Spanish? You know, like can you talk to people in two languages?"

"I only know a few words. I know some of the kids at school have people in their families who can't speak English. I guess everyone in my family can."

"It's good to know how to speak more than one language," he said.

"I guess," said Maricella. Then she started to think about the other children she'd seen the night before. "Jack, why weren't the two other girls at breakfast or lunch today?"

"Amber and Tamia? Oh, I forgot, you didn't get to meet them at dinner last night." He stopped and looked around the corner, then lowered his voice. "Daryl took them away last night right after supper."

"Where'd they go?" asked Maricella.

"What's all this whispering?"

Maricella jumped and saw Nina standing in the doorway. Funny how Nina could be so loud most of the time, but could sneak into a room when she wanted to catch one of the kids doing something she didn't like.

Maricella trembled. Tears stung her eyes as Nina grabbed her left arm and yanked her aside.

"You're supposed to be sweeping."

Jack stood up and moved closer. "She was waiting for me to gather up the big pieces of glass. Then she could sweep up the little pieces."

"Is that so?"

Her eyes looked evil, like the stories Mamá used to tell about the witch who wanted to eat little children, or the bad fairy who put a curse on Sleeping Beauty. Did this woman have those kinds of powers?

"Nobody told you to think for yourself. Since going to bed without supper didn't teach you a lesson, it's the closet for you."

"No!" screamed Jack. "It's not her fault. She's new here and is still learning the rules."

"Shut up, boy!" She backhanded Jack and sent him flying against the cabinets. Then she dragged Maricella through the house.

Maricella tried to pull away. "I'm sorry, I'm sorry. I won't do it again."

"Stop jerking around and begging. Jack says you need to learn the rules. Time for a lesson."

Nina opened a door Maricella had never been through and turned on a light. There were stairs going down. Maricella shook and started to sob.

"Please, please. I'll be good."

Not saying a word, Nina forced Maricella down the stairs.

It smelled terrible in the basement—like mud, only worse—and felt cold. Maricella saw shelves full of really dirty stuff. Old paint cans, a soccer ball, tools. Past them, she saw a door standing open. It was dark in there.

"Here's your new home," said Nina as she pushed Maricella inside where she fell to the rough concrete scraping her hands. "Have fun."

"No!" Maricella screamed, watching as the door slammed closed. She jumped up and tried to push it open. Then she heard laughter and something click.

"If you're good, I'll see about letting you out for supper. If I hear any more screaming, you can stay in there until suppertime tomorrow."

Again she heard Nina's heavy footfalls as she stomped away and climbed the stairs. Maricella heard the upper door slam and the faint sounds of Nina yelling at the Jack, telling him he could be next. Then Maricella moved slowly in this dark, smelly place and found something like a thin mattress to sit on. She had never been so scared. Pulling her knees up, she wrapped her arms around her legs and began to weep.

Chapter 13

Detective Kendall had called Brent to give him an update on the interrogation of Hector Fuentes. She indicated Fuentes might be telling them the truth about the Arroyo murder. His resources were excellent, and he probably knew exactly which of the Blood Brothers killed Javier.

Now all Brent had to do was find a Blood Brothers member who died a few weeks after the murder of Javier Arroyo, right? Of course, it couldn't be that easy. A total of four members were gunned down within two weeks of Arroyo's death, the murders taking place on three different days. It could have been any one of them. Now what would he tell Elena Arroyo?

"Sarge, you're still here," said Erica Barnes.

"Trying to tie up a couple of loose ends on the Javier Arroyo case. How was your day?"

"After you sent Flores off with Kendall, I decided to go through the evidence on the Arroyo case. I went over the ballistics report and then I took a walk down to Gangs. According to Manny Jones, the Blood Brothers most often use the kind of ammo that killed Arroyo."

"That makes sense. Kendall called in and said Fuentes implicated them. That's what I'm doing now. He'd only give us a clue about the timeframe. Unfortunately, there are four unsolved murders during this period of time. We'll probably never know which victim acted as the shooter in Javier's case."

"That's the problem. Nobody wants to talk. They're either too scared or too loyal. At least we know the killer is dead."

Brent ran his fingers through his hair. "How does Fuentes know he had the right guy? How do we know he's not messing with us?"

"We don't." Barnes walked over and put her hand on Brent's shoulder. "Why don't you try to relax? You and Natalie go out with Ben and I tomorrow night and we'll do drinks and dinner."

"My sister's in town."

Barnes rolled her eyes and then stared at him.

"What?" he said.

"Oh, I don't know. Uh, let's see, how many sisters do you have? Oh, yeah, three."

Now it was Brent's turn to roll his eyes, although he saw her point. "Brenda."

"I take it this was unexpected."

"Yeah, and I'm finding out Natalie isn't very excited about drop in visitors. I guess I never thought to say anything to my family because we've never run across anyone who made us feel like dropping in wasn't okay."

"Everybody's different, Sarge."

Brent let out a big sigh. "Things at home have been a little tense lately. I don't think Natalie truly understands my job."

Barnes sat on the edge of his desk, folding her hands in her lap. "What do you mean?"

"I'm supposed to be responsible for training new detectives, but she seems to think I should assign someone else to do it. Samuels is my first officer turned detective. I think she should be trained by a supervisor."

"So, she's jealous."

"I guess I shouldn't worry about it so much. She was a little jealous of you when we first started going out."

Barnes laughed. "Are you serious?"

"Yes, that is until she realized you already had a boyfriend. Then when I got the promotion and wasn't partnering up as much, I guess she didn't think I'd be working with women."

"That's ridiculous."

"I know it is, but that's why I sent Flores and Kendall to Michigan City today. When I mentioned going up there with Anne Samuels, well…let's just say she didn't seem very happy about it."

"Brent, you've got to understand a couple of things. One, you two have only been together for about eight months. You only recently decided to try living together. Two, she's an only child. No offense, but she's always been number one with her parents and had all of their attention focused on her. I bet she was an over achiever in school too, making her teacher's pet. I'm sure she expects the same kind of treatment from you."

"What does that have to do with my job?"

Barnes lowered her head and let out a strange, disgusted sound. "You can be really dense sometimes. Natalie doesn't know how to share you. She's looking at a cute young lady who is vulnerable, divorcing an abusive husband, and she knows how sweet you can be. You need to reassure her more than you would someone who had to learn to share growing up."

"I guess you're right. It's just…"

Brent's voice trailed off when Tyrone Mayhew came rushing toward him.

"Sergeant Freeman, we've got another one."

Chapter 14

"Parents are in the conference room in Missing Persons," said Tyrone as Brent followed him to the elevator. "They live on the far northwest side. Said their twelve-year-old daughter went to bed at around 9:00 p.m. When they got up this morning, the girl was gone."

"What makes you think this case is connected?" asked Brent.

The elevator doors opened and they entered. "A neighbor saw a dark colored minivan drive off. When I looked at the interviews from the Colon case, two of her neighbors had seen a dark blue minivan around the neighborhood that they didn't recognize. In addition, just like all of the other cases, someone went through the girl's closet and drawers and took some of her clothes."

Brent sighed. The latter clue was all too familiar. "I assume an Amber Alert has been issued."

"Yeah. Unfortunately, no one thought the person in the minivan was doing anything suspicious, so no license plate numbers," said Mayhew. "We put a description of the vehicle in the latest Amber Alert. I hope people will be more aware so they'll report minivans that don't belong in their neighborhood."

They exited the elevator and strode toward the conference room at a quick pace. Arriving there, Brent saw a crying woman wrapped in a man's arms. She must have heard them enter because she looked up and wiped her eyes.

"Mr. and Mrs. Myers, this is Sergeant Freeman. I've been

working with him on a similar case involving child abduction. I wanted him to be in on our discussion."

Mr. Myers rose and shook Brent's hand while his wife simply nodded. Brent and Mayhew sat in the chairs across from the couple.

"I don't want you to be alarmed, but I'm a homicide detective."

Brent's disclaimer didn't have the affect he'd desired. Mrs. Myers clenched her husband's arm, fear etched on every crease of her face.

"Unfortunately, I'm involved because the other missing girl's mother died during the kidnapping. We think she tried to stop the abduction. I don't think they'll harm the children because they took them for a reason."

Mr. Myers spoke as his wife continued to cling to him. "So, let me get this straight. They killed this girl's mother, but you think they won't kill the girl. What makes you so sure?"

Brent looked over at Mayhew whose sorrowful eyes told all. He then brought his attention back to the husband. "We're looking at this as a possible human trafficking situation. In the case I'm investigating, as well as your case, they took some of the girl's clothing and toys with them."

Mrs. Myers finally let go of her husband and leaned forward, twisting a tissue into pieces. "So they're going to sell my baby?"

Before Brent could answer, someone knocked on the door. Mayhew got up and opened it. A tall woman with flowing auburn curls stood there. Trish Zimmer, one of IMPD's favorite profilers, stepped into the room. Brent hadn't seen her since she helped them break the Emerson case and saved Erica Barnes's life.

"Special Agent Zimmer, it's good to see you again. I'm glad you could come so quickly," said Brent, offering her his hand.

"When you called yesterday and I heard there were child

abductions, I came as soon as I could."

Mayhew offered her a seat and introduced Agent Zimmer to the Myers. "Their twelve-year-old daughter, Haley, disappeared from their home overnight. Clothes and personal items were missing just like they were in the Colon case, as well as several other cases."

Agent Zimmer turned her attention to the Myers. "Is there any reason for you to believe Haley would run away?"

"Absolutely not," said Mr. Myers. "Our daughter is a very happy girl."

"Her birthday is in two days," said Mrs. Myers, choking on her words. "We planned to have a slumber party on Saturday night. She was so excited." Mrs. Myers broke down again, sobbing uncontrollably.

Reaching out, Agent Zimmer touched Mrs. Myers's trembling arm. "I know this is very difficult. I don't have any children myself, but I've seen a lot of parents go through this. We're going to do our best to bring your daughter home to you."

"But you can't guarantee it, or what shape she'll be in when she does come home," said Mr. Myers.

"There are no guarantees in life," she answered. "However, I can tell you while Haley is in the hands of this group, they won't harm her. They'll feed her and make sure she's healthy."

"Wouldn't want to damage the merchandise," Mr. Myers said bitterly. This only made his wife more hysterical. "I'm sorry, honey. I didn't mean it."

"I'm going to have some of my team come by your home today and look through Haley's room, if that's all right with you," said the agent.

"The police have already searched everything," said Mr. Myers, trying to comfort his wife.

"One of the things we look at is called victimology. We try to get to know the person who is missing to determine what attracted Haley's captors to her. This helps us develop a profile of the perpetrators."

Mrs. Myers lifted her head, her face red and twisted. "You have our permission to do whatever it takes. I want my baby back."

Chapter 15

Maricella sat very still on the stinky mattress. Her tummy ached because she had to potty. Without any windows, she couldn't tell if it was morning or night. It felt like she'd been in there forever.

Then a loud bang startled Maricella, causing her to wet herself. She'd probably be punished for this now, too.

"I told you never to put any of the children in that closet again, Nina." Maricella had never heard this woman's voice before. It was different, like she wasn't from Indiana.

"The girl wouldn't behave. I warned her."

Maricella heard something like when Papá smacked Mamá. Nina said something Maricella didn't understand. She wondered if this other lady was nice. She sounded very angry about Nina putting her in here.

"Shut your mouth, Nina. My father hired you to do a very simple job. This one's only five. I doubt she did anything vile enough to deserve this. If you can't control them without ruining them, you need to find another career."

"I think I'm doing a good—"

"Save it! Right now, you'll be very lucky if my father doesn't dispose of you for good. I'm assigning you to pickups, and you are not to discipline them any longer. Understand?"

"Yes."

"Good. After what you did to John, leaving us short of merchandise, I don't think you should be handling it more than necessary. Unlock the door."

As the door opened, Maricella put her hands up to her eyes against the light. It must be daytime. Then she trembled as she realized they would soon discover she'd had an accident. Instead, the lady bent down and took Maricella's hands away from her eyes. She was very pretty with black hair and a nice smile. Her eyes were brown, but shaped differently than anyone Maricella had met before. She'd seen people like her on television, but not in person. The woman offered her hand and Maricella took it.

"My poor, sweet girl. You've wet your pants. I'm so sorry for what Nina did to you. My name is Lin and I'm going to make sure you're taken better care of from now on."

They went upstairs to the kitchen where Lin turned to Nina. "Go upstairs and start a bath for this precious child. Make sure it's not too hot. I'll bring her up and bathe her myself in a few minutes. Oh, and make sure there are clean clothes in the bathroom for her."

Maricella trembled again at the angry look on Nina's face. She hoped Lin would stay so Nina wouldn't hurt her again.

"It appears I've told you my name, but you haven't told me yours," said Lin.

Maricella could hardly talk, because she was so thirsty.

"She probably needs something to drink," said Jack. Maricella hadn't seen him enter the kitchen.

"I think you're right, Jack. Please bring her a cup of water."

Jack glanced at her and then went to the sink. Maricella looked into his eyes and saw sadness. Wasn't he happy this nice lady came to rescue her?

After Maricella drank the whole cup of water, she finally felt able to speak. "My name is Maricella Maria Elizabeth Colon."

"That's a very long name. May I call you Maricella?"

Maricella nodded, but then her eyes widened as Nina entered the room.

"Her bath is ready," said Nina.

"Excellent. Now I want you to go down to the basement and clean out the nasty room. It smells horrendous."

"Come on, Jack...."

"No, Jack. You stay here and prepare a little snack for Maricella and then start dinner. Nina is going to do this task by herself." Maricella watched Lin's eyes narrow as she approached Nina. "You are the one who allowed the little closet to become what it is. You will clean it yourself. Am I clear?"

"Yes, Ms. Huang."

"Come, Maricella. Let's get you cleaned up."

Chapter 16

Brent yawned as he waited in the conference room for Detective Mayhew, the FBI agents, and his partner on this case to arrive. He hadn't slept well. It seemed like whenever he fell asleep at home, another nightmare would begin.

He tossed and turned every evening with dreams of children crying out in the night. Not just the abducted children, but also the Arroyo children. First, Javier stood before him, blood dripping from five gunshot wounds. He asked if Brent truly believed Hector's story about the Blood Brothers. In the next dream, he saw Lucia Colon on the floor, her skull crushed. She opened her eyes and stood glaring at him while speaking in a strange, far away voice. Why hadn't he found her killer and where was her baby?

Today he'd given up at three in the morning. He left Natalie's side, trying not to wake her as he went to take a shower. He'd removed his sweaty clothing, hoping the water would wash away his thoughts and fears. It didn't really help.

The door opened and Samuels walked in. She'd pulled back her mousy brown hair into a ponytail today, which made her look like a teenager. She carried two cups of coffee in her hands.

"Thought you might need this, boss. Cream and two spoons of sugar, right?"

"Thanks, Samuels. You're very intuitive. I didn't get much sleep last night."

"Neither did I." She placed her cup on the table and sat next to him. "I had nightmares about someone taking my boys. I can't imagine the pain of having your child just disappear."

"I'm not a father, and I can't imagine it. When you read the report from Kendall and Flores, did you feel Hector Fuentes was telling the truth?"

"I don't know.... It does seem kind of weird for him to come right out with it. Usually, if they 'take care of business' like he said, they don't admit it. Wouldn't that give us reason to continue to investigate his gang?"

"It does." Brent took a sip of coffee, mulling over her comments. "I think I'll have Flores and Kendall keep looking for a while. We still may hit a brick wall, but at least we can tell Mrs. Arroyo we tried."

The booming voice of Tyrone Mayhew made Brent turn towards the door. "Conference room's right over here, agents." Tyrone held the door open as two agents entered.

"Good morning, Sergeant Freeman," said Agent Zimmer. "I'd like to introduce Special Agent Nuwa Pan. She's an expert on human trafficking, and child trafficking in particular. She'll conduct the briefing today."

Brent rose and offered to shake her hand. Agent Pan wasn't as tall as Agent Zimmer. She had a pretty round face and shiny dark hair. "This is Detective Anne Samuels. She's assisting me on the Lucia Colon murder investigation. You've obviously already met Detective Mayhew, who is assigned the missing child's case."

"It is a pleasure to meet both of you," said Agent Pan.

"Please be seated, everyone," said Brent. "How did your time at the Myers house go? Did you find anything to give us a clue as to who's behind this?"

Agent Pan leaned forward, clasping her hands. Her intense brown eyes told of the seriousness of her coming words. "The girl is very pretty. At age twelve she would make a fine trainee for sale as a prostitute."

"I was afraid of that," said Mayhew. "They grab them when they're young enough to control. Do you have any idea where they might be taking these girls?"

Agent Pan leaned back in her chair, glancing to the side momentarily. "We've been investigating a group from China recently. They've hired people all over the United States not only for the purpose of prostitution, but to harvest organs for transplant."

Samuels let out a small gasp, and Brent sat back in his chair, dazed by this revelation. He'd heard of prostitution or even adoption, but harvesting vital organs? This would mean the child would die. No one spoke for what seemed an eternity.

The silence broke when Agent Pan continued. "I know it's shocking and relatively rare, but we think this group is harvesting vital organs from the younger children. They feel American children are well taken of and thus their organs are prime. The organs are shipped out of the U.S. because regulations here prohibit the purchase of organs from an unauthorized source."

"Why would anyone buy an organ from an organization like this?" asked Samuels. "How can they know it's a good organ or that it's sanitary?"

"They don't," answered Pan. "However, you must realize these are desperate people. Their child is dying and the wait lists are long. They'll do anything to give their child a chance at living."

Brent leaned forward, running his fingers through his hair. "So you believe this organization from China is linked to our kidnappings? Do you have any leads?"

"We do," said Agent Zimmer. "The task force headed by Agent Pan has been looking at someone here in Indianapolis. The woman's name is Nina Clemente. We had her under surveillance, but she shook our agents on the night Maricella Colon disappeared."

"We've been watching her house in case she showed up again," said Agent Pan. "She arrived this morning at 4:00 a.m. We thought you'd like to go with me to interview her, Sergeant Freeman."

"What about Mayhew and Samuels?" asked Brent.

"As I'm sure you know, we can't go barging in there with too many people. It might be easier to get her to talk if it's just the two of us."

"Okay," he said and turned to his partner. "Samuels, you stay here with Mayhew and go over what we have so far on the Colon case. Look for links between the kidnappings here in Indy."

"If I may, I'd like to consult with them as well," said Agent Zimmer. "I have some cases from other states we can go over, which we feel are related."

"Sounds good," said Brent. "Well, Agent Pan, shall we go?"

Chapter 17

"The twelve-year-old should be showing up at any time now, Father." Lin Huang sat back in her desk chair with a feeling of confidence.

"So, my daughter, were you able to take care of our issue with Miss Clemente?"

"Yes. I forbade her from handling the children any longer and sent her back to Indianapolis. I told her to wait there for further instructions on pickups."

"Lin, I do not think this woman will be satisfied with this. A handler makes more money. She will soon allow her greed to overtake her good judgment."

Dread swelled in her chest. "Then what would you have me do, Father?"

"I think you know this problem must be eliminated...permanently. Zeng Hu is on his way to take care of the matter."

"Yes, Father." She knew her father could be ruthless, but she also felt he was being much too hasty in his decisions to *eliminate* his problems. "I have Judy Klaussen coming to care for the children while I find a replacement."

"This is good. As a nurse, she can see to it the child comes to no harm. She will gain the child's trust, and then when the time comes, the little girl will not be hesitant to go with her to see Dr.

Sun."

"Thank you for your confidence, Father."

"Call me when you have a buyer for the twelve-year-old. From her picture, I can see she is quite beautiful and should bring a handsome price."

He disconnected before she could respond. She didn't like the business, but she was her father's only living child and she wanted to please him. Lin found the idea of these girls being bought for sex, and of little Maricella being cut to pieces as soon as they found someone who needed her organs, repulsive. Lin had to stay focused. She couldn't become attached to these young ones. She must think of them as property, not humans.

"Miss Huang."

She turned to see Jack standing in the doorway. "Yes."

"Daryl is here with another one. Should I help him with her stuff?"

"That would be very helpful. Haley is close to your age, so I expect you will get along very well. You will make sure she knows all of the rules and what happens when one disobeys, won't you?"

"Yes, ma'am."

A girl's screams rang through the house. "Let go of me! I want to go home!"

"This is your home now, girly. You ain't wanted by your folks no more."

"Bring her to me," said Lin. Jack nodded and went off to get the girl. He returned with her moments later, his hand firmly gripping her arm.

"Who are you people?" asked a sobbing Haley. "Why did you take me from my house? I want to go home."

"Silence."

Lin's voice was calm and stern, which stopped the girl from shouting, although tears continued to stream down her face.

"As Mr. Townsend told you, *this* is now your home. We bought you from your parents. They arranged for you to be taken in the middle of the night so none of your neighbors would see."

"That can't be true. My mom and dad love me."

Lin walked up to the girl and cupped her chin in her hand, raising Haley's head so their eyes met. "Not enough. They were tired of being your parents. They want to do things that are more exciting and fun. Things you prevent them from doing."

"I don't believe you. We were going to have a party for my birthday. They wouldn't do that if they wanted to get rid of me."

"Calling me a liar is not wise, young one." She tightened her grip on Haley's chin. "They planned this party to make people think they are innocent in all of this. There will be no more birthday parties for you."

Haley began to tremble. This was precisely the reaction Lin was hoping to see. Fear gave her the best control over the older children. She didn't have to strike them, simply create an atmosphere where the children thought her wrath to be fierce.

"Jack will show you to your room now. You will be sharing it with Maricella, who is a very sweet child and knows her place. I hope I will not find you have upset her in any way. Do you understand?"

"Yes."

"Come on upstairs then," said Jack.

Haley hung her head as she followed Jack up the stairs. A sign of defeat, but Lin would insist she be watched closely. Once she left to take care of business elsewhere, the girl might decide she was safe and try something stupid.

"Where's Nina?" asked Daryl.

Lin glared at him. "She has been…fired."

Daryl's eyes widened. Again, a perfect reaction. She not only had to have control of the children, she must retain control over the adults who worked for her father. This would guarantee her father's confidence and respect.

"Good. I'm glad you understand. As you know, it displeases my father when the merchandise is damaged. I hope you and Nina took proper care of disposing of John Balor."

"We did," he said. "Nina—"

Lin held up a hand, stopping him. "I don't need details. Daryl, moving the merchandise to another location is such a nuisance, and your farm has suited our needs. Not to mention the fact this has been very lucrative for you. Please be careful not to anger him."

"Oh, no. I appreciate everything ya'll have done for me. I woulda lost my farm if it wasn't for your father."

"You may go now," said Lin. She looked out the window across the vast acreage surrounded by woods. She smiled. It had been a good day.

Chapter 18

As he drove west on Washington Street, Brent felt a little uncomfortable with the silence existing between him and Agent Pan. Most of the women in his life talked continually. Of course, they'd just met, so maybe she felt this same discomfort.

"So, Agent Pan, how long have you been with the FBI?"

"I started my career ten years ago. I've been in trafficking for six years now."

"Then you know a great deal about human trafficking."

"Yes." She sighed and looked away. "Much more than I wish to know."

Brent nodded and gave his full attention to his driving as they approached the neighborhood of Nina Clemente's last known address on South Lyons. He came upon the surveillance team's vehicle parked three doors down and across the street from Clemente's house.

"Stop!" ordered Agent Pan.

Brent slammed on the brake, startled by her abrupt command. Following Pan's gaze, he looked over at the car and saw no one inside.

"Something's wrong," said the agent. "They were to stay in the car and report." She jumped out of Brent's car, leaving the door open.

He rolled down his window and watched as she peered into the vehicle. He saw her suddenly place her hand over her mouth. "What is it?" he called out, although he felt sure he already knew.

Ignoring his question, she returned to the car, took out her cell, and tapped in a number. "Yeah, this is Special Agent Pan. We need a team at the Clemente site. Two of our surveillance guys have been shot execution style. I've got a feeling we're going to find Nina Clemente in the same shape. The dead agents are parked in front of 1200, and her address is 1205." She paused. "Thanks. We're going to check the residence now."

Pan got in and slammed the door shut. "Let's go over to the house and see if she's still there. I can't believe they made our team." She looked out the window and her chest rose and fell as she breathed deeply.

"I'm sorry about your men," said Brent. He started forward, intending to park the car, when a black Mustang backed out of Clemente's driveway.

Agent Pan sat forward and pointed. "Follow that car. If it's not Nina Clemente, it's probably someone involved in what happened here."

"Do you want me to stop him?" asked Brent.

"Not yet. Let's follow whoever this is and see where he or she is going."

Brent picked up his radio and told dispatch they were following a suspect and would need backup. When they reached Washington Street, he told the dispatcher the suspect had turned west, heading in the direction of the Indianapolis International Airport.

He followed at least two car lengths back in the heavy lunchtime traffic. Almost losing sight of the car twice, Brent decided to get a little closer. That's when the Mustang accelerated and started weaving in and out, nearly sending people off the road. They'd been discovered.

Brent switched on his lights and siren and picked up speed while Agent Pan sat staring out the front window at their prey. He had to swerve to miss hitting an SUV whose driver didn't seem to understand he needed to pull over for a siren.

Gripping the steering wheel tighter, Brent saw the Mustang heading for the 465 on-ramps instead of continuing on to High School Road. These tight cloverleaf ramps needed to be taken at twenty-five miles per hour on a good day, so this might slow the suspect down. However, if he didn't catch up soon, Brent would lose him in traffic.

Brent punched the accelerator and took the on-ramp just five hundred feet behind his target. Then the Mustang slammed on his brakes.

Breaking much too quickly and moving toward the left shoulder, Brent hit a small patch of ice and started to spin out of control. Everything from this point on seemed to go in slow motion as he watched the Mustang speed off. Agent Pan's screams. Him gripping the wheel and taking his foot off the brake, trying to reclaim control. Going off the road and down the hill. Hitting an accumulation of snow and flipping. Then all went dark.

Chapter 19

"Unfreakinbelievable," said Anne. She walked away from Nina Clemente's house, the cold wind biting her cheeks. "We finally get a break in this case and somebody has to come along and kill our only suspect."

"Don't get too worked up, Samuels," said Detective Chennelle Kendall. "Our department has a pretty good solve rate, but we don't get them all. I know this is your first case, and we all want to show how good we are in the beginning. Just don't let yourself get discouraged."

"It wouldn't get under my skin so much if a little five-year-old girl wasn't still missing. I want her to come home to her grandmother. Mrs. Arroyo has lost enough."

"I know it's hard, Anne, but you've got to push your feelings aside. You can't afford to get too emotionally involved in your cases or you'll drive yourself crazy."

Anne's face warmed with a spark of anger. "How am I going to do a good job if I don't care?"

"I didn't say you shouldn't care, you just can't get too wrapped up in the emotions of the situation. How are you going to help people if you're not focused on the facts? When you decided to become a cop, this is what you signed up for. It doesn't matter if you're in homicide, gangs, missing persons, or on a beat. You can't lose focus."

Anne knew Chennelle was right, but this only multiplied her

feeling of frustration. Why did her first case have to involve a kid. It was tough enough dealing with adults' misery, but children were so defenseless. She shook her head to clear it.

"I'm sorry. I know you're only trying to help me. I'm glad I spouted off to you and not to Sergeant Freeman."

"Freeman would have understood. He's by the book, but not some macho jerk who thinks he's always right and everybody else is wrong. I've not partnered with him yet, but Erica Barnes did for several years. She says he's one of the best."

Anne didn't doubt it. The FBI had taken charge of this scene because two of their agents had been killed, so she had little to do. The last she'd heard, her boss and Agent Pan had gone off chasing the suspect toward the airport.

"You haven't mentioned Michael lately," said Kendall. "How's he doing since the *incident*?"

By incident, Chennelle referred to the fact that Anne's eldest son had to rescue her from his father's attempt to rape her. He'd found her Glock and had tried to scare her soon to be ex-husband when the gun went off, grazing Aaron's buttocks.

"He's doing really well," said Anne. "He and Jason go to therapy once a week. Their therapist is very pleased with how they're progressing. Of course, they have to deal with losing their grandfather, but living with my mother is helping all of us heal. She's always there when they are and she gives them loads of attention."

"I'm glad to hear it. How is your mom? Is she taking care of her own grief?"

"I think she's using her own brand of therapy—it's called spoil my grandsons and save my daughter."

"I hear you."

"So how are things going with Trevon?" asked Anne.

Chennelle's eyes saddened. "So far, so good. At least it seems like he's behaving himself. I'm still struggling with the trust issue though. Once trust is broken, I'm not sure you can ever get it back."

Footsteps put a halt to their conversation. Agent Zimmer walked toward them at a rapid pace.

"I just received a phone call from Major Stevenson. Detective Freeman and Agent Pan were involved in an accident while chasing down the subject. They were taken to IU Health Methodist Hospital. I assume you know where it is."

Anne's heart rate rose and she could barely think. "Are they okay?"

"He didn't have any details. They slid on an on-ramp at 465 and Washington Street. The car rolled once before coming to a rest."

Chennelle pulled her keys from her purse. "Well, then, since they don't really need us here, let's stop wasting time and get down there."

Chapter 20

Voices. He heard lots of voices. Sirens? He'd heard sirens. Not now, but there had been sirens…when? He was trying desperately to open his eyes, but they wouldn't cooperate. Brent could feel pain…his head…what happened? Why couldn't he open his eyes?

More voices…he knew they were voices. He couldn't understand them. Were they talking to him or someone else? Confusion. So confused. So tired. Maybe he should simply give in and rest.

Someone called his name. "Sergeant Freeman. Sergeant Freeman, can you hear me?"

He tried again to open his eyes, but his eyelids were so heavy. Why doesn't she let him sleep? Yes, the voice belonged to a woman, but who?

"He's starting to respond to verbal stimuli, Detective Barnes," said a female he who's voice he didn't recognize. "That's a good sign. I have to check on my other patients. I'll be back in a few minutes to check on his progress."

Brent tried to call out to Erica, but only felt a deep rumble in his throat. Had he said something? Why couldn't he make his body do something? He pulled his eyelids harder and thought he caught a fuzzy glimpse of brown hair.

"Hey, you lazy bum," said Erica. "Look at me when I'm talking to you."

He tried again. It was hard. His head hurt. Brent raised his arm and could see his hand begin to come into focus a little at a time. Dazed and confused, he let it drop and closed his eyes again.

Then he heard a bang and rapid footsteps. "Erica, thank you for calling me. Is he okay? Is he awake?"

At the sound of his twin's voice, Brent tried to respond.

"He's trying to wake up. He's been out for a while now. The doc has ordered an MRI. Wouldn't want anything to be wrong with that sweet little noggin of his."

"You're so funny."

The touch of Brenda's hand gently brushing his hair from his forehead finally did the trick. Blinking a few times to try to focus, he saw his sister smiling down at him as her hand rested on his cheek.

"Hey," Brent croaked.

"Hey," said Brenda, tears forming in her eyes. "How are you feeling?"

"Lousy...I've got a headache."

Brenda laughed and wiped away a tear. "At least you haven't lost your sense of humor."

"He's got a sense of humor?" quipped Erica.

"Can it, Barnes." He winced at the attempt to laugh along with two of his best girls.

"The doc says you can't have pain meds until they do the MRI and assess the damage," said Erica. "Now that your sister's here, I'd better get back to work. I'll check on you later. Oh, and I almost forget, the Honda is toast."

"Great," he said.

Erica opened the door and nearly knocked over Agent Pan. Brent was glad to see her walking around, although he didn't know how she accomplished it. She went to the side of the bed opposite Brenda.

"Sergeant Freeman, you're awake. I'm afraid our suspect got away."

This seemed to be an attempt at humor, but he didn't feel like laughing. Not about this. "And Nina Clemente?"

"I just spoke to Agent Zimmer. Nina Clemente is dead, and so are the two agents in the car. Agent Zimmer, Detective Samuels, and Detective Kendall were at the scene, but your detectives are on their way here now. This is definitely an FBI case now, but we want to continue to work with your police department to find the Colon child."

"Detective Samuels will assist you in my absence, but I need Detective Kendall to work with Detective Flores on another case right now. I should be up and ready to go in a couple of days."

"Whoa there, bro. Let's get your MRI before you start making plans to go back to work." Brenda gave him her take-charge look, the one where her brow furrowed and her eyes got all squinty. Then she pulled her gaze from her brother and introduced herself to Agent Pan.

He tried to ignore his sister and focus back on Agent Pan. "I'm much tougher than my darling sister seems to think I am. By the way, can I assume since you walked in here fully clothed you're doing okay?"

"Yes, they told me we were fortunate we only rolled once. The fact I'm so short, and my seat had been set so far back from the airbags, kept me from being injured more severely. The airbags kept me from banging my head on anything, but they told me I could still have a mild concussion from my head-jerking around in the roll. I've got seat belt bruises of course, along with a couple of nasty ones on my legs and a few cuts on my hands from flying glass. But other than that, I'm fine."

"Sounds like enough—"

The door flew open, interrupting his last words. Kendall and Samuels entered this time. Both wore frowns on their faces that turned to smiles as they approached him.

"Sergeant, you had us worried. I'm so glad to see you're awake," said Kendall. She patted his leg gently.

"He's not out of the woods yet," said Brenda. "He just woke up about ten minutes ago."

"Yeah, when I heard my sweet sister's voice," said Brent. "Ladies, let me present my womb mate, Brenda Freeman, veterinarian extraordinaire."

"I didn't realize you had a twin sister," said Samuels.

Brenda looked at him with wide-eyed shock. "I can see why you wouldn't want to talk about our two older and very mean sisters, but I would have thought you'd be bragging about me."

"It's not like that, Brenda. Samuels just came off of patrol a few days ago. She and I haven't had a chance to get to know each other yet."

"Well then, I forgive you."

All the ladies started to laugh and Brent grinned, his head still throbbing. Most men would love having four beautiful women surrounding their sick bed. However, at this precise moment, Natalie walked in.

Chapter 21

"Time to take your blood pressure, Mr. Freeman." Brent's nurse pulled the blood pressure cuff over his arm and started the annoying procedure.

Brent knew why people complained about being in the hospital and not getting any rest. They must have awakened him a dozen times overnight. He supposed this had to be done because of his concussion. At least the tests they'd run showed no fractures, hematoma, or significant swelling in his head. Those airbags *were* good for something.

"Any way I can get something for the pain this morning?" he asked.

"I'll check your chart as soon as I've taken your vitals. Once the doctor evaluates you this morning, it's very likely you'll be going home."

"That sounds good...." He peered at her nametag. "...Susan."

Footsteps brought his attention to the doorway. Agent Trish Zimmer and Anne Samuels entered and asked the nurse if they could talk to Brent for a few minutes.

"Sure, as soon as I'm finished." Susan looked at Brent, her one eyebrow raised. She stuck a tympanic thermometer in his ear. "You did hear me when I said you'd be *going home*, right? Not back to work?"

"Yes, ma'am," he said.

"Good. He's all yours, ladies. I'll check on those pain meds for you, Mr. Freeman."

"Well, Samuels, you didn't anticipate your first case would have you working with one of the FBI's top profilers, did you?" asked Brent. He tried to sit up and winced. Not only did his head still throb, but he couldn't determine what part of his body didn't hurt.

Samuels smiled at him, but her eyes held pity. He hadn't looked in a mirror lately, but could just imagine the bruises the airbag had left on his face.

"Thanks for the compliment, Sergeant Freeman. I take it you're doing better?" asked the agent.

"I am, but it could be a few days before I can come back to the office. Of course, it doesn't mean I can't be consulted at home from time to time."

"I've ordered Nuwa to take a couple of days rest as well. Agent Pan may not have been as badly injured as you, but her muscles are giving her fits this morning. Do you think I could drop her off at your place tomorrow with a laptop so the two of you can at least talk through what we have so far?"

Brent remembered the look on Natalie's face when she walked into his hospital room yesterday with him surrounded by four pretty women fussing over him. Well, three if you didn't count his sister. He doubted Natalie saw her as a threat. However, working with Agent Pan in their home might put her over the edge. In any case, he couldn't say no.

"No problem." He gulped. "Did you find any clues at the Clemente scene?"

Brenda walked in at that precise moment with Susan by her side carrying precious relief in one hand.

"I'll have Agent Pan brief you tomorrow. Today you need to rest," said Zimmer.

"That's right, bro," said Brenda. "According to your nurse, the doctor will be looking over your chart in a few minutes and you'll be getting out of here. I've come to escort you since Natalie had to be in court today."

The nurse approached and gave him the cup of pills. "The doctor said you can have two Ibuprofen every four hours. You can't have anything stronger due to the concussion. You'll want to call your primary physician if you have any problems, but it looks to me like you have a great team here to look after you. Let them help you."

Brent nodded and downed the pills with some water.

"See you at your place tomorrow morning," said Zimmer as she left the room.

"Glad to see you're okay, Sergeant," said Samuels. "I'll keep you informed if we find anything new."

"Thanks, Anne."

Once Anne and the nurse were out the door, Brenda pounced. "Before you zone out, what happened after I left last night?"

Brent looked away. He really didn't want to get into this with her.

"Do you honestly think I didn't see the look on Natalie's face and feel the tension in the air? You could have cut it with a knife."

There wasn't any point in his trying to hide it, not from his twin. Although they weren't identical, they were very close. One could sense when the other was unhappy, hurt, or angry.

"Well, she wasn't very happy to find me being fawned over by a group of women. Since she didn't seem to want to talk, I closed my eyes and tried to sleep. Then I heard her make some snide comment about being the last to know."

"It was a little difficult for any of us to get hold of her yesterday since she had to be in court." Brenda's face turned pink

78

like it did every time someone upset her. "As a matter of fact, she was in closed chambers with a judge. Were the rest of us supposed to stay away until she got here?"

Brent sighed and closed his eyes. The meds hadn't taken effect yet, making it hard to think past the pain in his head.

"Brent, I love you. You and I aren't just siblings, we're best friends. As your best friend, I've got to tell you I think you rushed into moving in together too soon. I don't think you'll be happy spending the rest of your life with someone this jealous."

"Brenda, please."

"Not facing it doesn't mean I'm not right." She pulled up a chair and leaned in, taking his hand. "As long as you're with her, I will always treat her with respect and kindness. My question to you is, how long can you stay with her when you can't even do your job without worrying about how Natalie is going to react? There are three women and one man on your shift in Homicide right now. Are you always going to be able to partner with him to keep Natalie happy?"

"I love her."

"I know you do." Brenda paused and rubbed his hand between hers. The pink in her cheeks had faded, but her eyes bore a sadness he hadn't seen since their father died. "Sometimes loving someone doesn't mean we can develop a good relationship. Don't forget our mom loved our dad. Remember how miserable she was?"

"This is different," said Brent. He couldn't understand how she could make such a comparison.

"Only in what he did to make her so unhappy. Unhappy is unhappy."

Oh man, he hated it when she was right—especially when he didn't want her to be. He couldn't deny Natalie had seemed more possessive since they returned from their cruise last month. Her reaction to him spending so much time with his new detective had been ridiculous, as well as her jealousy of his partnering with Erica Barnes when they first met.

"You look tired." Brenda gently stroked his temple with her fingers. "How's your pain level?"

"It's getting better." He paused, closing his eyes, enjoying the tenderness that reminded him of their mother. "I think I'll take a nap."

"Sounds like a good idea. I'll drop this subject for now. Just know I'm here anytime you need to talk about things. And I won't tell Mom."

She stood still, holding his hand with one of hers. He felt her gently brush his hair back from his forehead and kiss it as he faded into slumber.

Chapter 22

Detective Flores leaned back in the passenger seat as Chennelle settled into the driver's seat of her sedan. "One of my buddies in the Gangs Unit gave me this name. He said if anyone from the Blood Brothers knew what happened, Dwayne does. He'll be hanging at Thirtieth and College."

Chennelle started the car and put it into gear. "I guess it's better than nothing," she said. "Seems like these gang types take care of business their own way."

"That's what makes it so hard to solve a gang related case," said Flores. "When we'd get a good idea of who did the deed, he'd end up on a slab. That's why so many of those guys working gangs get numb to all the killing."

"I hear you," said Chennelle. "Just one big vicious circle. It's too bad so many innocents get caught in the crossfire."

"Yeah, that's the hard part. One of the guys used to say we should tell them to come in and give them shooting lessons so they actually hit their intended target instead of just firing in hopes of getting the right guy."

"What's really sad is to see those friends and family on camera begging for the killer to turn himself in. Most of the time they're trying to reach people who only care about themselves. If the shooter really cared, he wouldn't be running around with a gun in the first place. None of it's right."

"I'm with you there. The hardest part about working in the

Gangs Unit is keeping everybody straight. There used to be a nice hierarchy about them. You had a head honcho, his lieutenants, and on down. In today's 'got to have it now society', the ambitious don't wait to work up the ranks. They just go out and create a new gang. There are hundreds of factions now."

Chennelle turned the corner onto College Avenue. "Thirtieth and College coming up. You seen this guy before?"

"I've seen pictures. He'll be the one with the Colts coat and hat. Dwayne's six-four, so I bet he'll be easy to spot."

As they pulled up to the corner, Chennelle spotted Dwayne. He had a couple of buddies with him, but they were only about six foot tall. Chennelle parked, turned off the engine, and got out of the car. She waited for Flores. As they approached the gathering, she saw Dwayne roll his eyes and glance around. Good snitches did this sort of thing to keep their companions from finding out what they were really doing.

"What they want?" asked one of Dwayne's friends.

"Don't know. Maybe they just need to ask what time it be." Dwayne smiled at them, his gold front tooth gleaming against his dark lips.

"How you doing, Dwayne?" asked Flores. "We heard you've been selling H in front of the grade school again."

"You've got the wrong man, officer. I don't deal drugs to no little kids."

Chennelle watched friend number one snicker and put his hands in his pockets. In turn, she loosened the snap of her Glock holster.

"You two make yourselves scarce," said Flores.

The boys looked at one another and then at Dwayne.

"Go ahead and tell Zeke I'm detained. No use you standin' 'round here gettin' hassled too." Dwayne moved his head to the right and they left in that direction. When they'd moved out of earshot, Dwayne turned to Flores and spoke in a low voice.

"I been told you're looking for the Javier Arroyo shooter. I can tell you right now it weren't no Blood. That boy weren't no gang member. Blood don't waste time shootin' people outside'a the gangs. Understand?"

Chennelle listened as Flores questioned Dwayne since he had more experience dealing with gangs than she did.

"I do, but why would Hector Fuentes say it was a Blood and go after a Blood for doing the deed?"

"He playin' wit you. Who he say did it? Never mind. You wouldn't be out here talkin' to me if you knew, right?"

Flores glared at Dwayne. "Right. So nobody from the Blood Brothers who died within a week or two after the Arroyo kid was shot had anything to do with it?"

"Thing is, lots of our brothers die all the time. If Los Hombres does the killin', they brag on it. And they don't hold back on the reason, neither."

"Are you sure?"

"I ain't got no reason to protect a dead man," said Dwayne. "If it had been a Blood Brother done it and a Los Hombres took out revenge on him, I'd know it."

Screeching tires caused Chennelle to turn around. The only thing she saw was the semi-automatic before a burning sting pierced her left shoulder, sending her to the ground. She heard Flores scream for them to get down and felt something warm spatter her cheek. Shocked and dazed, she fumbled for her gun, but the car was speeding away before she could get a shot off.

The flame in her shoulder grew worse. She found her radio and called for assistance before she stumbled over to check on the others. Dwayne was slumped against the wall of the store, his eyes open in a death stare. Flores just a few inches away lay on his back with a bullet hole in his neck, coughing up blood.

"No, no, no," she cried as she made her way to her partner. "Flores. Flores, you hang in there, you hear me? Don't you leave me."

Chennelle used her right arm to pull Flores closer. She could feel the blood and saliva from his mouth soaking her shirt, but she wouldn't let go. She rocked him like a child.

Now she could hear sirens. "You hear that, Tomas? They're coming. They're going to help us and you're going to be all right. They're coming."

She spotted the patrol car first and saw Officer Donovan Bays jump out of it. He waved at someone in an arriving ambulance. Chennelle continued to rock Flores. She could barely make out what Bays said to her until he cupped her chin in his hand and looked her in the eye.

"Detective Kendall, you need to let go of him now. The paramedics are here and they'll take care of him."

One of the paramedics gently extracted Flores from her. Officer Bays helped her stand and she saw another ambulance pull up. She looked down to see her clothing soaked in blood. She couldn't determine if it belonged to her or Flores.

"Detective, were you shot? It looks like there's a bullet hole in the left shoulder of your coat," said Bays. "I'm going to take you over to that ambulance so they can take care of you."

Chennelle planted her feet, stopping abruptly. "No, no, they have to take care of Flores. He's much worse than I am."

"Don't worry, there are two ambulances here. The other paramedics are taking care of Detective Flores. Right now, we need to take a look at this shoulder wound. You need to be taken care of as well."

"I can't leave him, Bays. He's my partner. I have to make sure he's okay."

One of the paramedics from the second ambulance touched her right arm. "The best way you can take care of him is to take care of yourself. Isn't that what he'd want?"

She looked into his kind green eyes and nodded, allowing Bays and the paramedic to help her into the back of the ambulance. Bays stayed with her while the paramedic did a preliminary exam of her shoulder.

"I recommend you let us take you to the hospital so a doctor can take a look at this," he said as he applied a thick dressing to the wound.

"Looks like more patrol cars are out there now, so I'd better get back," said Bays. "I'll check on you later, Detective."

Bays jumped out of the vehicle and walked toward the scene. Chennelle stood up to see past him. The first responders were picking up their equipment. Flores lay still on the ground, piles of bloody gauze, paper, and plastic tubes all over the sidewalk. Dizzy, she nearly fell, but the paramedic caught her and laid her on the gurney. He closed the back doors, strapped her in, and she began to weep.

Chapter 23

"Haley, I want you to meet Maricella," said Lin. "This young lady stayed in my room last night but will be sharing your room from now on."

Maricella looked at Haley curiously. She looked like a nice girl, but sometimes the older girls at school were mean to her. She looked to be Jack's age.

Lin led Haley over to where Jack stood. "Jack, I want you to show Haley where things are in the kitchen. She will be setting the table for breakfast this morning. I have some phone calls to make, so I will see all of you later."

Maricella watched as Jack showed Haley where all of the dishes, glasses, and silverware were stored. He'd already pulled out everything she needed for this morning's breakfast. "Maricella, could you help Haley set the table? I have to keep stirring the gravy and keep an eye on the biscuits."

Maricella nodded and grabbed the plates, placing the silverware on top. Leading Haley into the dining room, she didn't speak until they arrived at the table. "We have to make sure the dishes are on the placemats because they don't want the table to get scratched. Same with the silverware and glasses. I'll go back and get those."

Haley started putting out the plates and Maricella ran back to the kitchen. Coming up behind him, she tugged on Jack's shirt. He turned his head towards her.

"What's up, Mari?" He'd given her this nickname and she liked it.

"Do you think she's a nice girl?" Maricella asked.

"Don't know. When she got here yesterday, she was kind of upset. Most of them usually are. Of course, if she gives you any trouble, let me know." He winked at her and went back to his stirring.

Maricella smiled and began taking glasses in two at a time. Her hands were too small to try carrying more. Only five people would be at breakfast this morning since Nina left: Lin, Haley, Jack, Daryl, and her. By the time she'd brought in the fifth glass, Haley had finished her part.

"So I get to share a room with you," said Haley. Tears started to run down her cheeks. "I want to go home. I don't want to be here."

Maricella felt bad. She knew exactly how Haley felt. "I'm supposed to have a birthday party this weekend. My mom wouldn't plan a party and then give me away."

"Shhh," said Jack quietly. He looked around before setting a bowl of hot biscuits on the table. "If they hear you talking about it, you'll get in a lot of trouble."

Haley stomped her foot. "This isn't fair."

"I told you to shut up." Jack tried to keep his voice down, but he looked really mad. "Lots of things aren't fair. None of us kids want to be here. Those people tell all of us the same story, so I expect it isn't true, but what can we do?"

"We can run away."

"Do you have any idea where we are?" said Jack. He got closer to her and spoke quietly. "We are somewhere out in the hills of Kentucky in the middle of winter. Even if we could get out of here, no tellin' how far we'd have to walk to find another person. And there are bears in those hills and it gets dark early and is really cold with all the snow we got." Jack eyes became wild. "Besides, Daryl says wolves and coyotes are out there, too. Sometimes he sees wild cats. In this weather they'll be really hungry."

"How do you know he isn't lying?" asked Haley. "Maybe he's just saying that to keep you from running away."

"You're impossible." Jack turned and went back to the kitchen.

Haley followed him, so Maricella decided to do the same. He tipped the skillet to pour the gravy into a large bowl.

"Why won't you answer my question?" asked Haley.

Jack slammed the pan down on the stove. "Daryl's lived here all his life. All I know is that I grew up in the city. He's only taken me hunting a few times. I don't know anything about where those woods end, and it can be dark and scary, especially at night. I do know I never seen any neighbors, 'cause he never lets me go out past the tree line."

"Why don't you sneak out to the road and put a letter in the mailbox telling the mailman to help us?" asked Haley.

Maricella thought this was a really good idea.

"Because if I get caught, Daryl will beat me within an inch of my life," said Jack. "Lin gave me to him as a reward for doing such a good job and letting them keep us here. He's really mean when you upset him."

Maricella hadn't seen that side of Daryl. She'd only been punished by Nina. She shivered at the thought of Daryl taking over the discipline. Her Papá was mean, too. He would be really nice to her and then hit her for no reason.

"You'll get used to it, Haley," said Jack. "We all do eventually."

Jack grabbed the bowl of sausage gravy and took it into the dining room. Maricella and Haley turned as they heard someone come in the back door.

"Breakfast ready yet?" asked Daryl.

"Yes," said Maricella, shaking. "Everything is on the table. I think Jack went to tell Lin."

"Good, I'm starvin'. Well, don't stand there gawkin'. Get in there." Daryl shooed them into the other room like he shooed the chickens.

Lin and Jack were standing next to their chairs.

"I hope the three of you have become acquainted," said Lin. "I'm sure you'll be good friends as long as you remain our guests here. Now let's have some of this delicious breakfast."

Chapter 24

"I'm doing alright, Mom," said Brent. "Believe me; my car is in much worse shape than I am. I'm just glad Agent Pan didn't get hurt badly."

Brent jumped as he heard a cabinet door slam. Natalie must be listening to his phone conversation. She wasn't very happy last night when he told her he and Agent Pan would be working together in the apartment today. Brenda's words kept ringing in his ears. "Unhappy is unhappy."

"Son, it doesn't matter if you're five or seventy-five, you'll always be my little boy and I'll always worry about you."

"Brenda will be in town a couple more days. I know she'll be keeping tabs on me for you."

"I might buy it of one of your older sisters; however, Brenda's always been very protective of you. It must be the twin thing."

Brent laughed and heard another cabinet door slam. Natalie came into the living area and grabbed her coat out of the closet. With briefcase and purse in hand, she left without saying goodbye, slamming the door behind her.

"What's all that noise?" asked his mother. "Is she tossing your crap out the door?"

"Don't be silly."

She sighed. He knew that sigh. It usually meant he wasn't

fooling her, but she'd given up on pressing him.

"Okay, sweetheart. I'll call you in the morning to see how you're doing. Love you.

"Love you too, Mom."

He placed his cell phone on the table and rubbed his eyes with the heels of his hands. Only seven-thirty in the morning and he was already tired. He'd had a hard time trying to get comfortable in bed last night. The Ibuprofen helped his headaches, but he needed something more for the rest of his battered body. Natalie finally got tired of his tossing and turning and suggested he take one of her Vicodin so he could sleep. It did help him until she got up and started banging things around.

The added stress about what happened to Flores and Kendall yesterday wasn't helping his pain. It was bad enough when a cop was killed, but when it was someone in your department on your watch, it was worse. This left his shift three detectives down. Major Stevenson must be pulling his hair out.

A knock on the door brought him back to the present. He opened it to find Agents Zimmer and Pan waiting outside. Opening the door wider, he gestured for them to enter.

"Is it still okay for Nuwa to be here today?" asked Zimmer.

"Sure," said Brent. "I'm doing okay. The headaches are better and I'm feeling pretty good." Not exactly the truth, but he didn't want her to think him incapable of working today.

Zimmer set a computer bag on the coffee table. "I'll be back to pick up Agent Pan at eleven o'clock unless you decide to quit before then. Nuwa, please call me if you need to leave sooner."

"I will, Trish," said Agent Pan.

The door closed and Brent took a deep breath, trying to relax. Agent Pan pulled out her laptop and grimaced. She must be experiencing some muscular pain as well. Nobody came out of an accident like theirs without feeling it for weeks.

"Major Stevenson made some changes in your absence. Detective Samuels will no longer be assisting us. He assigned her to work with Detective Barnes on the murders of Detective Flores and Dwayne Glover. He said your cold case would have to wait unless it ties in with what happened yesterday." She paused, looking down at her hands. "I'm sorry about your detective, Sergeant."

"Thanks." He hadn't even had the chance to spend any time with Flores and now he was dead. "I'm sorry about your men, too."

She nodded. "The major also considered bringing Jin Osaka up from nights to assist the day shift. With what happened to Detective Flores, and with you and Detective Kendall out, he's really shorthanded. I heard Detective Kendall is doing well, but she'll be out for about six weeks."

Brent sighed and put his head in his hands. Why did everything have to happen all at once? In light of his work situation, his problems with Natalie seemed minor.

"Are you okay, Sergeant?" asked Nuwa. "I can call Agent Zimmer if you aren't feeling up to this today."

He sat up straighter. "I'm good. Do they have anything on the Clemente case yet?"

Nuwa typed on the computer and then turned to Brent. "Nina Clemente died on the scene of a single gunshot wound at the base of her skull. Sounds like a pro to me. Your medical examiner said she died instantly as the blast severed her spinal cord. FBI forensics took over and turned her place upside down looking for clues of her involvement in this trafficking ring. They couldn't find a cell phone, so we think her killer took it with him."

"Can't we get a record of her calls?"

Agent Pan frowned. "Unfortunately, we can't find any records of Nina Clemente owning a cell phone."

Brent flushed with disbelief. "Everybody has a cell phone."

"I'm sure she did. However, she either bought a disposable cell or took it out under an assumed name. My bet would be on the disposable."

Rising, Brent paced from one side of his living room to the next while rubbing his temples. The rush of blood to his brain from this frustrating news made his head ache again. His shoulders and back tensed up as well. He could sure use another dose of that Vicodin, but he needed to be clear headed right now.

"Did they find the Mustang at the airport?"

"The plates we called in were stolen from another vehicle, but they checked all of the rental car companies and those who had Mustangs didn't have any with the paint color we described."

"Great." He heard her tapping away at her keyboard again.

Nuwa frowned at what she saw on her laptop. "We don't think he went to the airport. A pro like this would have used a private plane of some sort. Nobody left Indianapolis International Airport during the hours after the accident. We've had it staked out in case this man stuck around and planned to leave when things cooled down. The more likely scenario here is he simply left town and used another airport. There's a BOLO on the car, but we lost precious time getting the information out due to our accident."

"So where do we go from here?" he asked.

"Clemente is as close as we've been in a long time. We start digging into her life. People like her usually do the grunt work. They're the ones who always make mistakes. We'll find something."

"I don't know how you do it," he said. "You've already been working on this trafficking ring for years. Why do you keep doing it?"

"For the children."

Chapter 25

Anne watched new snowfall as she and Erica Barnes drove to the hospital. Since Detective Kendall wasn't under the influence of any post-surgical narcotic painkillers, they needed to interview her about the shooting.

"You've had a pretty rough initiation into Homicide," said Detective Barnes. "How you holding up?"

"I'm fine. I just feel bad for Chennelle and for the Flores family."

Barnes sighed. "It's always rough losing one of our own. This is going to be extra rough on his family since it's so close to Christmas. He had a wife and three kids."

The thought almost brought tears to Anne's eyes, but she took in a deep breath to stop them. She wondered what would happen to her two boys if she were to die in the line of duty. The Flores children still had their mother, but Michael and Jason would have no parent with their father in prison and their mother dead. Anne closed her eyes and thanked God for her brothers and her mother, any one of whom would care for her boys.

When she opened her eyes, she noticed Barnes slowing down and getting ready to pull into the hospital parking lot. When the car stopped, they exited in silence and didn't speak again until they were inside the building.

"Do you remember her room number?" asked Barnes.

Anne pulled out her notebook, which she would need when they reached the room. "It's 4415B."

They rode the elevator to the fourth floor and found the room easily. A nurse came rushing out of the room and Anne almost ran into her.

"How's she doing today?" asked Barnes.

"Physically, she's doing very well," said the nurse and then lowered her voice. "I'm concerned about her mental state. She's not conversing much, won't watch TV, and stares at the wall or out the window a lot. Her friend, Detective Adams, has been here night and day. I think he's worried, too. He just went down to the cafeteria for some breakfast."

"Thanks," said Barnes. "We'll try to cheer her up."

Anne knew Detective Barnes was only humoring the nurse. What they'd come to talk to Chennelle about wouldn't cheer her up. Of course, if she felt involved in catching the killer, it might bring her out of her funk.

"Hey, girl. It's good to see you're awake," said Barnes with a little too much verve.

Chennelle had been staring out the window, but turned her head at Erica's voice. Normally, this tall slender woman looked like a fashion model, but not today. Her dark complexion could not hide the circles under her sad eyes. The smile she usually bore had vanished. The nurse had given them a precise diagnosis of Chennelle's mental state.

Chennelle picked up her control and made the head of her bed rise to a sitting position. "You two on the case?" she asked.

"Yeah," said Barnes. "With the sarge out for a couple of days, Major Stevenson decided to put our rookie with me on this one. He figures the FBI can work with Freeman on the Colon case. Besides, they've got Mayhew helping with the kidnapping end of it."

"What's going to happen with all the new cases?" asked Chennelle. Then her eyes filled with tears, her face contorting with pain.

Barnes touched Chennelle's uninjured arm. Anne grabbed the tissue box off the side table. She couldn't think of anything else to do. She'd only known Chennelle Kendall through the few times they'd met at crime scenes. Without being told, she decided she'd take the notes and allow Detective Barnes to ask the questions.

Now, rubbing Chennelle's right shoulder, Barnes waited to speak until the crying ceased and Chennelle had wiped her face. "Chennelle, I know this is hard, but we need your help to find whoever did this to you and Flores."

Chennelle nodded. "I don't remember much, because I had my back to the street. Gang territory and I had my back to the street. How stupid was that?"

Anne saw tears form in Chennelle's eyes again; however, Erica Barnes's skill at bringing Chennelle back amazed her. Another great mentor from whom she could learn.

Sounding more like the Detective Kendall Anne knew, Chennelle closed her eyes and started recounting what happened. She and Flores had barely started talking to Glover when she heard a vehicle. She'd turned around, seen the semi-automatic, then felt the shot hit her left shoulder, knocking her to the ground. It had all happened so quickly she didn't get a good look at the shooter. The black car was huge, like a Lincoln, but she couldn't get a plate number.

"I know it's not much," said Chennelle. "When I went down, I heard Flores shout. The next thing I knew his blood...." She couldn't finish and the pained expression returned.

"Detective Barnes," said Trevon Adams, walking into the room. The tone of his voice and the scowl on his face weren't very welcoming. "You really need to be doing this right now?"

"You're a cop, what do you think?" said Barnes.

"I think Chennelle's been through enough."

In spite of Detective Adams being a prime jerk, Barnes simply smiled at him then looked back at Chennelle.

"I only have one more question for you. Did Glover give you any useful information on the Arroyo case?"

Chennelle closed her eyes again then opened them. "I remember him saying no Blood would have done it, because Arroyo wasn't a gang member. He said that he'd have known if there'd been retaliation."

Barnes patted Chennelle on the hand. She looked up at Trevon. "We've got her statement, and I think she did remarkably well for what she's been through. She's a pro."

Anne waited for Adams to give Barnes a sharp retort, but Chennelle shook her head at him. This silent signal stopped the conversation.

"We'll take off now," Barnes said to Chennelle. "I'll check on you later…as a friend. No more questions, but you know the drill. If you think of anything else, you know where to find me." Then she squeezed Chennelle's hand and actually got her to smile.

Anne said goodbye and followed Barnes out the door. They walked a few feet down the hall in silence and then Barnes stopped abruptly. Anne nearly rear-ended her.

Barnes seemed frustrated. "That jerk thinks he knows my partner better than I do. It's all I could do not to put my fist in his smug face."

"I think he's just feeling protective of her right now," said Anne.

"Possessive is more like it." Barnes shook her head. "Anyway, it looks like you and I are destined to get in the middle of this gang thing, like it or not. They're all going to be on high alert since a cop's been killed."

"So do you think this case is solvable?"

"Every case is solvable, Samuels. Some are just harder than others."

Chapter 26

As Maricella helped Haley clean the bathroom, she heard a knock at the front door. She looked at Haley, who shrugged. They heard Lin welcome someone named Judy. Maricella wondered if this woman would be staying instead of Nina.

Throwing down her sponge, Haley motioned for Maricella to follow her. "Let's go to the top of the stairs and listen. Maybe we can find out who she is."

Maricella wasn't sure about this plan, but her curiosity got the better of her. Besides, how bad could the punishment be? Lin sent Nina away because she hurt her. However, Maricella wasn't sure she could really trust Lin.

"We can only go down six steps, because the seventh one creaks," whispered Haley. "Stay behind me. If we hear them coming we have to hurry back to the bathroom as quiet as we can."

Maricella nodded. Lin might not be so generous to Haley if they got caught.

Haley stopped on the sixth step and Maricella on the fifth. Lin and Judy were in the room with the desk, but hadn't shut the door.

"I am sure you've heard Nina is no longer in our employ," said Lin. "She didn't treat the children well."

"That won't do," said Judy. "Prices will go down."

"We want them to behave, but there are other more suitable

methods, if you know what I mean."

Maricella heard a snorty laugh she assumed came from Judy.

"Don't worry, Ms. Huang, I've been a pediatric nurse for fifteen years. I know how to keep children fit and healthy *and* get them to behave without physical cruelty."

"I'm glad you see my point," said Lin. "I want you to do a thorough physical exam of the five-year-old. An opportunity to harvest has come our way. Desperate parents make the best customers."

Haley looked up at Maricella with a scared face. It took her a moment to realize they must be talking about her, the only five-year-old in the house. The word harvest made no sense to her, and desperate parents? She started to ask, but Haley put her index finger to her lips and Maricella closed her mouth. A feeling of dread washed over her, although she wasn't sure why.

"Your room is on the second floor at the top of the stairs," said Lin. "Why don't you go up and settle in. I'll introduce you to the children at dinner."

Maricella heard chairs sliding across the floor. Haley pointed toward the bathroom and they scampered back as quickly as they could. She hoped they were quiet enough.

In the bathroom, Haley slowly closed the door. She grabbed Maricella's arms, startling her, and spoke in a whisper. "You can't tell anyone what we heard, understand?"

Maricella didn't understand why, but she nodded.

"We have to talk to Jack, but we can't do it in the house. I don't want Lin or this Judy to know we heard them."

"But...."

Haley cut her off before Maricella could speak. "No buts, little girl. I think what they said was really bad, but I think Jack can help us. He really likes you and seems to want to protect you. He's our only hope."

"We have to help him tomorrow with the chickens."

"You're pretty smart for a runt." Haley smiled at her, but Maricella thought she looked sad.

"Come on. Mari. We'd better get done here in case Judy needs to freshen up."

Chapter 27

"Thanks for coming in today, Mr. Washington," said Detective Barnes. "Since one of your members, as well as one of ours, was shot in the street, we thought this would be safer for all of us."

Anne sat next to Barnes taking notes. Jamal Washington, the head of the Blood Brothers, had agreed to come to the department to talk with them. He was tall, dark, and intimidating. The man was a work of art, literally. Although dressed for the cold weather, he showed tattoos on his hands and down all of his fingers, up his neck and on his left temple. She suspected his upper right arm bore two hands clasped and dripping blood—the Blood Brothers official tattoo.

"So, what can I do for you fine ladies?" he asked.

"Know anybody who wanted Dwayne Glover dead?" asked Barnes.

"They's a lot of hate out there. 'Course you know dat."

"Okay, Jamal, I don't have time for this crap. Either you know or you don't. Which is it?"

Jamal smiled at her and leaned back in his chair. Anne couldn't believe Erica could hold her temper, because *she* wanted to knock him of his chair.

"It's like this. He was losin' friends in the Blood. People suspected him of workin' on something with the cops. Then one of my crew said they saw him with a Hombre. Now that don't sit well, if you know what I mean."

"So are you telling me you did this?" asked Barnes.

"Nah, nah, nah," said Jamal with an irritating lilt to his voice. "I'm just sayin', his time was getting short. 'Course, if Los Hombres found out he was workin' with one of theirs, they might not be happy either."

"So, basically what you're telling me is, you have no idea." Barnes's statement reflected a hint of impatience. She glared at Jamal until he responded.

Smirking, Jamal nodded and stared back at Barnes for a moment. "Now you're getting' it. Don't know, don't care."

"I've got something else to ask," said Barnes. "We got word one of the Blood Brothers did the Javier Arroyo killing a couple of years ago. Know anything about that?"

He crossed his arms and leaned his chair back on two legs. "Hmm, I seem to recollect that one, but no Blood touched that boy."

"How can you be sure?"

"Because he weren't no Hombre. We ain't goin' around killin' innocent people."

Barnes pursed her lips. Her annoyance was showing and Anne wondered if this interview could reap any benefit.

Leaning forward, Barnes glared at Jamal. "What about the two-year-old who caught a bullet when your boys did the old drive-by two weeks ago, and the nincty-year-old woman who died when bullets from your crew came through the wall of her home three weeks ago while she and her family were eating Thanksgiving dinner? Or the preacher who died last week when one of your boys gunned him down trying to get to an Hombre who was talking to him? Weren't those innocent people?"

"Accidents happen."

Anne was right. She was glad they hadn't risked getting shot to talk to this uncooperative guy on the street. His non-answers were cold and full of contempt for the law. However, Anne did remember Chenelle telling them Glover had said the same thing about Javier Arroyo. No reason to kill someone who wasn't a member of Los Hombres.

"Okay, Mr. Washington, I think we've heard enough," said Barnes. "You're free to vacate the premises."

"Thank you, ladies," he said. "Always a pleasure helpin' Indy's finest."

Once she'd seen him to the elevator, Barnes came back into the room and kicked her chair. Anne had been writing down some final notes and practically fell out of hers.

"I hate talking to gang members," shouted Barnes. "They are the most arrogant, rude, unfeeling…." She slammed her fist on the table, causing Anne to jump again.

"Sorry, Samuels. I'm just so angry. They always hint that it's the other guy, not them. I hate going in these circles. I can't imagine ever working in the Gangs Unit."

"Did you catch the connection to what Dwayne Glover told Detective Kendall and what Washington just said about the Arroyo case?"

"Not at the time, but you're right. Good catch. Good to see Freeman hasn't ruined you."

Anne laughed nervously. She didn't think it wise to insult her boss, but she knew Barnes had been Sergeant Freeman's partner for many years and sarcasm had become a standard part of their relationship.

"So what now?" asked Anne.

"I think we're going to have to ask for some assistance from Gangs. Did Kendall say who Flores contacted?"

Anne leafed through her notes from their conversation with Chennelle. "No."

"I'll find someone. Thank God the weekend is coming."

Anne nodded in wholehearted agreement. As Barnes had said earlier, it had been a rough week.

Chapter 28

Anne sat in the living room of her parents' home watching the lights twinkle on their five-foot spruce. It was a small tree, but one she and her mother could manage with no men around to haul something heavier. They and the boys had chosen their favorite ornaments from her mother's stock. A smaller tree meant fewer ornaments.

"Beautiful, isn't it?" said her mother. She sat down next to Anne on the couch and patted the top of her thigh.

"Yes. It's just sad that Dad isn't going to be here to share it with us." Anne wiped away a tear, remembering how a drunk driver killed her father less than a month before. They'd already had to miss Thanksgiving with him. A stab of resentment went through her as she thought about the woman who killed him being out on bail and home with her family for the holidays.

"I know what you're thinking, Anne. I know it's really fresh for all of us, but harboring hatred for her only hurts you and trickles down to Michael and Jason."

She looked at her mother in disbelief. "How can you be so forgiving? Dad worked one of the most dangerous jobs for over thirty years without a scratch. Then he retires from the force and this happens."

"I loved your father more than words can say. The only way I can get through losing him is to remember where he is now. He'll actually be able to say happy birthday to Jesus in person."

Her mother always did know how to put a positive slant on things. Anne knew anger to be destructive, but with the pain so fresh, letting go seemed impossible.

"Christmas is just a few days away." Her mother also had a knack for changing the subject if things became tense. "Have you finished your shopping?"

Anne wiped away her last tears and leaned forward. "I need to get a few stocking stuffers for the boys, and I still don't have anything for Grant. It's a hassle shopping for him."

"Your brother does like to play golf. Why don't you get him a gift certificate from the club pro shop where he plays golf?"

"Mom, I wind up doing that every year. It would just be nice to buy something different."

"You talking about our pain in the tushy brother?"

Anne turned to see her brother Jeff standing in the doorway smiling like a Cheshire cat. He had a few gifts in his hands, which he deposited under the tree.

"Yeah," said Anne. "Did you figure anything else out?"

"Actually, my lovely wife came up with a brilliant plan."

"Do tell," said Anne.

"She suggested we combine Grant and Melody's gifts this year and get them a gift certificate to their favorite restaurant and include a promise to babysit for them so they can have a romantic evening together."

"Can I pitch in on it?" asked Anne. She saw him smile at the desperation in her voice. He'd done that since they were kids, and it irritated her as much now as it did then.

"Sorry, Sis. Camille already bought the certificate."

"Why don't you buy him a gift certificate to the wine store

where he and Melody shop?" suggested her mother.

Jeff sat down next to his mother and wrapped his arm around her shoulders. "Are you trying to turn our beloved elder brother into a wino, Mom?"

His mother scowled at him and smacked him lightly on the chest. Then all three of them started laughing.

"Uncle Jeff!" yelled Jason. He ran up and plopped himself in Jeff's lap. "Did you bring any presents for us?"

"Maybe."

"Get out of Uncle Jeff's lap, you big baby," said Michael as he strode into the room.

"Michael!" said Anne. "That's enough."

"Well, he is too big to be sittin' in people's laps," Michael protested. Then he spotted the new gift boxes.

Before he could look at them, Jason shoved him out of the way and went for them. Anne was about to shout at them for their rowdiness when her brother interceded.

Jeff grabbed his nephews around their waists and picked them up like sacks of potatoes. He nearly tripped picking up Michael. It seemed he hadn't considered how much Anne's elder son had grown.

"All right, you two," said Jeff. "Do not be getting on your mother's nerves this close to Christmas or some of this stuff just might disappear."

Jeff put them down and instructed them to apologize to their mom and grandmother. When they finished their apologies, Jeff wrestled them to the floor and proceeded to tickle them.

That was it. The last straw. Anne jumped off the couch and turned on her brother. "You're worse than they are!" Then she bolted out of the room toward the kitchen. She heard her mother tell the boys to get up and come sit next to her.

Intending to get a glass of water, Anne turned on the faucet. Instead, she leaned against the sink and burst into tears. The next thing she knew, her brother came up behind her and wrapped his arms around her. She turned and buried her face in his shoulder. Then she realized he was crying, too.

"It doesn't feel right," she said.

"No, it doesn't." Jeff stroked her hair and continued to hold her tight. "I had so much I wanted to tell him."

Jeff had been the stereotypical middle child, always the rascal, always the athlete, always the one vying with the others for Dad's attention. Grant had been the scholar and Anne the baby girl, so where had this left Jeff?

Anne pulled away and grabbed two paper towels. She wiped away Jeff's tears then gave it to him. They both blew their noses rather loudly before starting to laugh.

"You look like crap," he said.

"So do you. Maybe we should splash some of this cold water on our faces since the faucet is still running."

"Sure," he said and nudged her so he could go first. Anne pushed him aside as they laughed and wound up splashing water all over the place.

"Children!"

Her mother must have come into the kitchen to investigate all the racket. Anne and Jeff turned to see their mother flanked by Michael and Jason, who had their arms crossed and wide grins on their faces.

Anne and Jeff looked at one another then hung their heads and said in unison, "Sorry, Mom." Then everyone, including their mother, was laughing.

The phone rang and Anne raced Jeff to it, grabbing it before he had a chance. She giggled as he tried to take it away.

"Stop it, this could be work," she said. Anne held the earpiece to her abdomen so the caller wouldn't hear the commotion.

Her mother came up and gave Jeff a little whack on the arm and he stumbled over to the boys acting as though he had been mortally wounded. They, of course, exploded into laughter.

"Out of here, all three of you," said her mother, shooing them like a flock of geese.

Once the rowdies left the kitchen, Anne lifted the receiver to her ear. "Hello, I'm so sorry for the delay. To whom am I speaking?"

A moment of silence made Anne think the caller had hung up during the shenanigans, but then she barely heard a low masculine voice. "Detective Samuels, I'm only gonna say this once. If you know what's good for you and your lovely family, you'll forget about the Arroyo case. I hope you understand what I'm saying." The line went dead.

Slowly she took the receiver away from her ear and stared at it. Stunned at first, she slowly realized she and her family had just been threatened. If this man knew her home phone number, he probably knew where she lived.

Jeff came back into the kitchen. "Those boys of yours.... What's the matter? Did you get bad news?"

Anne hung up the phone, turned to him, and smiled. "No, just a wrong number."

Chapter 29

"Come on, Mari," said Haley as she pulled on her snow boots. "This is a really good time to talk to Jack where no one will hear us. We can help him feed the chickens. Just let me do the talking, okay?"

Maricella nodded. She didn't know what to tell Jack anyway. The stuff Haley kept saying scared her. Harvesting must be a bad thing or Haley wouldn't want to talk to Jack alone.

They trudged through the new fallen snow. Maricella stepped into Haley's footprints to keep as much snow out of her boots as possible. She didn't want her feet to get cold. Haley still wanted to run away, but how could they make it with so much snow on the ground?

They finally reached the chicken coop to Maricella's delight. She knew it would be warm in there. Daryl had to use heaters because chickens don't have any fur to keep them warm like the cows and horses did.

Haley opened the door. "Hey, Jack. Is it okay if we help you?"

"Sure, but don't stand there with the door open. You're letting all the heat out."

They walked in, Maricella closing the door behind them and stomping the snow from her boots.

"Why would you want to come out in the cold to help with this?" he asked.

"Maricella and I are city girls. We've never been in a chicken coop before."

That was true. Maricella had seen the chickens outside when she arrived, but hadn't seen them since the snow started. Looking around at the nests on different shelves, she wondered how the birds knew which nest to sleep in.

"Really?" said Jack. "I don't think Mari will be much help. She can't even reach them."

"She can watch and learn, or hold the basket for me."

"Okay, Haley. What's the real reason you came out here?" asked Jack. "I hope you're not on that running away kick again."

Maricella knew Jack wouldn't fall for Haley's city girl story. She hoped Jack wouldn't be mad at her for going along with it. He looked out for her and she didn't want him to stop.

Haley moved closer to Jack and lowered her voice. "I have to talk to you about something Mari and I overheard yesterday." She then went into how they heard Judy arrive and then sat on the stairway listening to Lin and Judy's conversation. When she got to the part about harvesting, Jack looked at her funny.

"Are you sure that's what they said?" asked Jack.

"Yes, I swear it," said Haley.

Jack walked back and forth, shaking his head and chewing on his finger just like Maricella remembered her mamá doing if she got nervous about something. She would walk around and sometimes yell at Maricella for no reason. The little girl decided she would just be quiet and see what Jack said about this harvesting thing.

Jack stopped abruptly and shook his finger at Haley. "You can't tell anybody else about this, you hear me."

Haley nodded. "That's why I'm coming to you."

"Did they say when?"

"No," said Haley. "They just talked about getting her ready. Making sure she was in good health because of how somebody named Nina had treated her."

Maricella thought Jack might be getting a headache. He put both hands on the sides of his head and rubbed it. He looked scared. Maricella could feel her own heart beating faster at his reaction. This must be really bad.

Jack finally stopped rubbing his head and lowered his voice, pulling Maricella and Haley closer. "Now here's what we're gonna do. Mari, you don't say anything to anybody about this. You do what you're told, but if anyone says something about taking you on a trip, you let me or Haley know, okay?"

Maricella nodded. She didn't really understand, but knew this must be very important.

"Haley, listen to conversations whenever you get the chance. Don't go standing outside of doors or you might get caught. If you hear them talking about a date, let me know."

"What are we going to do if they decide to do it now?" asked Haley.

Jack walked in a circle and then made a weird noise like a growl. "I can't believe this is happening right now. We've got to keep watching the weather for a break and hope it comes before they decide to take her."

Maricella wanted to cry. Nina and Daryl had already taken her from her mamá. Wherever Lin and Judy wanted to take her now must be really horrible if Jack was thinking of helping her get away.

She couldn't help herself any longer; Maricella had to ask the question. "What's harvesting?

Jack took her gently by both upper arms. His eyes were very

sad. "Mari, I don't want you to be scared. Me and Haley will think of something. We won't let anything happen to you."

He didn't answer her question, but Maricella trusted Jack. When he said he'd take care of her, she knew he meant it. She'd just have to pray. Abuela Elena said prayer was the answer to all our hurts. Maricella had to trust God would help Jack and Haley to save her.

Chapter 30

Brent fumbled with his burgundy linen napkin, nearly dropping his silverware on the floor. He hoped this was his normal klutziness and not a result of the Vicodin he'd taken before he left the apartment. He didn't hurt right now, but he didn't want anyone reporting him as incapable of going back to work.

"Coordinated as ever, I see," said his former partner, Erica Barnes.

"Give the guy a break," said Ben Jacobs. "I think he's doing great for only being out of the hospital a couple of days."

"Ben, Ben, Ben, you know what it's like to be razzed by a fabulous and quirky partner," she said. "Freeman here is used to it. If I didn't give him a hard time, he'd think I'd lost my mind."

Natalie sat silently glaring at Erica, who seemed totally oblivious to the darts coming her way. Brent couldn't understand where Natalie's sense of humor had gone. She'd been reluctant to accept this invitation to dinner, but caved in when Brent told her he was going crazy sitting around the house. Apparently her concession didn't mean she had to have a good time.

"Don't worry, Ben," said Brent. "I just ignore most of what she says. Selective hearing. You may want to give it a try now that the two of you are living under the same roof."

Before Erica could retort, the waitress brought their drinks and took their food order. Natalie excused herself to go *powder her nose*.

"Don't you have to go to the bathroom, too?" Erica asked Ben.

"No, not real...oh, yeah, I kinda do. I'll be back shortly."

"That was subtle," said Brent.

"I guess. I need to tell you something before Nat comes back and I figured since it's homicide I'd get Ben to take a hike, too."

"Please don't call her that, she hates it."

"I'm not real concerned about her tender feelings right now, Sarge. I'm worried about our rookie detective."

"Why, has she screwed up already?"

"No, she's great," said Erica. "Samuels called me this afternoon to tell me she got a call from some guy who threatened her and her family if she didn't get off the Arroyo case."

"Seriously?"

"Yes. He told her if she knew what was good for her and her family, she'd forget about the Arroyo case."

"Something's not right here."

"Ya think?"

"Why would somebody be so worked up over a case this old? Do you think it's the same guy who shot Kendall, Flores, and Glover? It starting to look like no one wants us to solve the Arroyo case."

"I'm beginning to think so. When Samuels and I talked to Jamal Washington, he told us the same thing Glover told Kendall and Flores, no Blood Brother would have killed Javier Arroyo."

"So basically, Washington is telling us Hector Fuentes is steering us in the wrong direction."

"Would it surprise you?" asked Erica.

"You two aren't talking shop, are you?" asked Natalie as she slipped back into her seat next to Brent.

Brent could feel the blood rushing to his face. It seemed lately Natalie took every opportunity to embarrass him.

"I confess," said Erica. "I insisted on giving Sergeant Freeman a quick update, but we're done. Now he can be plain old Brent again."

"I miss anything?" asked Ben, breaking the tension as he returned to the table. He gave Erica a quick shoulder squeeze.

She smiled and looked up at him. "Not really. Just letting the boss know he's left his unit in capable hands."

Ben leaned over and kissed her cheek. "Of course he did. You'd better get that noggin of yours back to normal soon or this one might take over." Ben took his seat. "Where's the food? I'm starving."

Brent snickered at the look Erica gave Ben. Her right eyebrow raised in a manner you knew meant she thought you were a dope for what you just said. A familiar look he missed since becoming shift supervisor.

"So when are you coming back?" asked Ben.

"I go see the doctor bright and early on Monday morning. If he releases me, I plan to come into the office right after."

"Brent, you should take it easy for a few more days," said Natalie. "I know your shift is short handed, but you won't be much good to them if you relapse."

Tired of her mothering and hovering, Brent lashed out. "How do you relapse from a concussion, Natalie? Just because I lost consciousness for a short time doesn't mean I'm brain damaged!"

"I...I...didn't...." Natalie had become speechless. "I'm just concerned you'll go back to work too soon," she whispered.

Brent continued, his frustration raising the volume of his voice to the point where people were staring. He didn't care. Now Natalie could be embarrassed. "I can't go back to work too soon. Sitting around the house doing nothing, knowing not only are we shorthanded, but our caseload is growing. And now one of my detectives has been threatened. The least I can do is go back to work and sit at my desk where I have all the tools I need to coordinate things."

"Please lower your voice," said Natalie. Her face grew redder by the minute. Whether from embarrassment, anger, or both, Brent didn't know, and at the moment it didn't concern him.

"I'll lower my voice, but I'm going to tell you this for the last time. I'm going back to work on Monday. I know Erica is qualified to do this job, but I need her in the field. Unless the doctor gives me a good reason, I'm going back to work."

Natalie started to open her mouth, but Brent held up his hand. Even Erica stayed silent, and she usually always had something to say. Of course, he knew she'd never seen him lose his temper like this.

The food arrived and conversation ceased while they all dove into their meals. Brent ate his steak as though he hadn't eaten in weeks, but the argument had the opposite effect on Natalie. He noticed she was mashing the insides of her baked potato with a little too much enthusiasm while barely touching her grilled chicken. Of course, she refused dessert. He could have eaten something more, but he noticed Ben and Erica also said no to dessert, so he refused as well. Apparently, they were ready to end this evening as quickly as possible.

When Ben pulled up in front of the apartment complex, Natalie exited the vehicle without so much as a goodbye. He knew he'd be sleeping in the guest room tonight, but he was still angry with her and with his circumstances, so it was probably better anyway.

"Sorry about my outburst tonight," said Brent.

"Holy crap, Brent, I've never seen you get so hyped up," said Erica. "I kind of liked it."

"Can it, Barnes." Brent smiled at her and she smiled back. "Guess it's time to go face the music. I wish it was Sunday instead of Saturday. Tomorrow won't be fun."

"She'll get over it once she's had a good night's sleep," said Ben. "You know, once she thinks about it for a while I'm sure she'll see you're just stir crazy. A guy like you needs to be doing something."

Brent liked Ben for his optimistic attitude, but knew Natalie well enough to expect a day of misery until he apologized.

"Let's hope so," said Brent. "Thanks again for bringing the car and for driving tonight."

As he got out of the vehicle, Erica rolled down her window. "See ya, partner."

"See ya."

Chapter 31

The doctor had told Brent he wanted him to ease back into his job. This meant desk duty for at least three days. Feeling a bit fatigued already, he decided to follow doctor's orders and perhaps work half a day. The first order of business was to get his detectives together and find out where everyone stood in their investigations.

When he walked into the office, he found the bull pen empty. Surely they hadn't gone out in the field when he'd specifically told them he wanted to meet with them at ten. He decided to check the conference room.

When he opened the door, the word *SURPRISE* bellowed from many voices. A banner that read *Welcome Back Sarge* hung on the wall. A tray of cupcakes sat on the table, and he smelled freshly brewed coffee. Looking around the room, he saw Detectives Samuels, Barnes, and his temporary detective, Jin Osaka. Then he saw that Detective Mayhew from Missing Persons and his boss, Major Stevenson, were also in attendance.

"Thanks everyone," he said. "I didn't expect such a big welcome after only being out a few days."

"Well you didn't think we'd pass up an excuse for goodies, did you?" asked Barnes. He loved her wicked smile.

Tyrone Mayhew grabbed two cupcakes in his large right hand and then patted Brent on the shoulder with his free hand. "Glad to see you back, but I have to get back up stairs. Hopefully, this second cake will make it to Jacobs's desk."

"Good to see you. Anything new on the little girl?"

"The FBI has taken over, so I'm off the case. We have too much going on right now for me to argue," said Mayhew. "The agents should be here pretty soon to go over things with you. See you later."

"Since I haven't had the chance to update you on new assignments, I hope you don't mind if I sit in on this meeting, Sergeant," said Major Stevenson.

"Of course not, that would be great," said Brent.

"Good to have you back, son." Stevenson slapped Brent on the back, sending a sharp pain through his left shoulder where the seatbelt had bruised him. Brent nodded at his boss, hoping his pain didn't show on his face.

Barnes approached with a cupcake and coffee in hand. "Here you go, Sarge. Sugar to get you going and coffee just the way you like it—fresh." She looked around then lowered her voice while setting his treats on the table. "How did things go with hurricane Natalie yesterday?"

Before he said anything, he pulled out an unlabeled bottle and took a Vicodin with a swig of coffee. "Actually, Natalie went to visit her parents in Evansville yesterday, so I had a very quiet day. I went to bed before she returned."

"Interesting," said Barnes. "Brent, you're one of my best friends, and I want you to be happy. At the moment, I'm seeing way too much misery. Are you sure you want to continue this relationship?"

"Right now, I just want to find out what everyone has been doing and dig into my work." He didn't want to cut her off like this, but he also didn't want anyone in the room to overhear. Whatever he said to Barnes would never go any further, but he wasn't so sure about some of the others.

"Maybe later," she said. "And what was that you just popped in your mouth? It didn't look like Ibuprofen."

Brent cocked an eyebrow to signal he wasn't going to answer her. Then he raised his voice over the din. "Okay, everyone. Take a seat so we can go over things and get back out there."

He started by introducing Jin Osaka. "For those of you who don't know him, Detective Jin Osaka has agreed to work day shift to give us a hand since I'm on the desk for a few days and Kendall is out. If we treat him *nice*, maybe he'll love us so much he'll transfer in and third shift can have the headache of finding someone new."

After everyone finished laughing, Brent asked Major Stevenson to bring them up-to-date on case assignments.

Major Stevenson gave a report on new cases. A merchant was killed in an apparent robbery attempt and he'd assigned it to the Robbery Division even though it involved a homicide. They would report findings directly to him for the time being. Osaka's case involved a woman whose body turned up in the Garfield Park area. Barnes and Samuels were still on the murders of Flores and Glover.

"We're waiting to hear from Detective Flores's family regarding funeral arrangements," said the major. "We understand they're waiting to hear from some of his family in Mexico before they're able to set the date. In all likelihood, it will happen after Christmas. It's always hard to lose one of our own, but I know he'd want us to carry on."

After a moment of silence, the major took his seat and Brent continued. "Thank you, Major Stevenson. It has come to my attention there is an odd turn in Detectives Flores and Kendall's investigation into the allegations made by Los Hombres leader, Hector Fuentes, regarding who actually killed Javier Arroyo. At first, we thought Flores and Kendall simply got caught up in the gang war between Los Hombres and the Blood Brothers—wrong place at the wrong time. However, Detective Samuels received a threatening phone call this weekend from someone who told her to back off of the Arroyo case."

Anne's face turned red. Perhaps she hadn't thought Barnes would report this to him so quickly, but Brent had to put everyone on alert.

"It's bad enough we've lost one detective and have one in the hospital. Whoever is behind this is making threats to do more of the same. It appears Dwayne Glover may have had information someone out there didn't want him to share about the Arroyo case. Everybody on this shift should be particularly vigilant. We just need to find out what the connection is."

Barnes raised her hand and Brent acknowledged her. "Just so everyone knows, Samuels and I talked to the leader of the Blood Brothers, Jamal Washington. For the most part, he's the uncooperative jerk we expected. However, he did say nobody from the Blood would have had reason to kill Javier Arroyo. Even if a gang member shot him, it doesn't make sense that a person even mistaken for a gang member would cause this type of response."

"Detective Samuels is new to Homicide," said Major Stevenson. "How would he know she's on this case? And why choose her to threaten?"

"Because I'm new," said Samuels. "Maybe he thought he could scare me. I'm not saying I'm not scared for my kids and mom, but the question is, how did he get my personal information?"

"Could there be someone at the P. D. involved?" asked Barnes.

Brent had the same thought. How else would this person know to target Samuels and be able to get her home phone number?

"Are you okay with continuing on this case, Samuels?" asked Brent.

"I have to be, otherwise, this will set a precedent for other criminals to do the same thing."

"We're very lucky to have you, Detective Samuels," said

Major Stevenson. "We'll see about having extra patrols go past your mother's house."

"Thank you."

Someone knocked on the door. Barnes opened it to find Agents Zimmer and Pan.

"Good morning everyone," said Agent Zimmer.

Major Stevenson rose. "Sergeant Freeman, I think you can handle things from here on. I need to return to my office."

"Osaka, you're dismissed. I'll be in the office if you need me," said Brent. "Barnes, you and Samuels can stay. I have a feeling there's more of a connection between these cases than we thought."

Chapter 32

Agent Zimmer opened her file and looked around the table. "To give you a profile on these traffickers is easy on the one hand, difficult on the other. The reason being, this is something they do for money."

"They treat the children better than their own," said Agent Pan. "They feed them, try to keep them calm, and tell them lies about their parents' motivations. The younger the victim, the quicker trust will be established with the captor."

"We think Nina Clemente broke the rules," said Zimmer. "We did a check on her and she lost her own children a couple of years ago due to abuse and neglect. I doubt she nurtured these children the way her employer expected."

"So they killed her," said Brent. This didn't surprise him.

Agent Zimmer nodded. "That's what we think. In *this* business you don't get fired, you get eliminated. The bosses can't take a chance you will turn into a *disgruntled ex-employee* who might contact the police."

"Why did they hire her?" asked Samuels. "Don't they do some sort of background check?"

"Maybe they chose her because she does have a criminal past," said Barnes. "They probably thought the money would inspire her to do what they told her to do."

"That's a good theory," said Zimmer. "Some people talk a

good game to get what they want, but eventually their real behaviors surface."

Agent Pan leaned forward, elbows on the table and hands clasped. "One thing we're concerned with is the fact more and more gangs are getting involved in human trafficking. We need to find out if Nina Clemente was affiliated with a local gang in some way. I think this is even more important now that I've learned that Detective Samuels has been threatened."

"I agree," said Brent, although he wasn't sure how the human trafficking could tie in with the Arroya case. According to Arroyo's mother, the boy was spotless. He could just see Elena Arroyo's reaction if he suggested these incidents could be connected.

"What can we do to help?" asked Barnes.

Brent stood and ran his fingers through his hair. "Your main focus has to be on finding out who killed Flores and shot Kendall, and what Glover knew that made him a target. If you have to go into the neighborhood, take a couple of patrol officers with you."

"You've always got our back, Sarge," said Barnes.

Her grin gave him the impression she wasn't taking this seriously. "I mean it, Barnes. When people start shooting and threatening our detectives, it's time to step it up a notch."

Barnes's facial expression said it all. "Okay, okay. I didn't mean for you to think I'm taking this lightly. I'm sure I'm speaking for Samuels as well when I say we don't fancy getting shot."

"You need to find out who Flores spoke with in Gangs," said Brent. "See if they can shed any light on Glover and why someone would go after him. And, ask them who's in charge of Los Hombres with Fuentes in prison."

"We're meeting with Detective Jackson today," said Barnes.

"I should have known you'd be one step ahead of me." His eyes met Erica's and she gave him the faint smile which generally meant she felt bad for him. Their ability to communicate without words stemmed from several years of being partners. Sometimes he missed being out there in the field with her. Right now, he felt like a pressure cooker about to explode.

"Okay, Barnes, you and Samuels can go now," he said. "Be aware when you talk to them that if there's a cop involved in this, someone from that department would be a likely candidate. After all, whomever Flores asked about the Arroyo case would have known about the meeting. Let me know when you talk to Jackson and what he says about Glover."

The two detectives rose and were almost to the door when Barnes turned to Agent Zimmer. "It's always good to see you, Trish. Are you going to be here much longer?"

"No, actually I'm leaving after this meeting. I'm needed back in D. C. Agent Pan can take it from here."

"Have a good trip," said Barnes as she and Samuels exited.

Brent remembered that when FBI profilers were finished giving the local police what they needed, they generally moved on. Then if there existed a need for an FBI presence, another agent would be assigned. In this case, that agent was human trafficking expert, Nuwa Pan.

Brent sat down across from the agents and Zimmer continued. "Your team will have some hard roads ahead. These types of organizations are ruthless and hard to catch." She got out of her chair and collected her things. "I leave you in Agent Pan's capable hands, Sergeant. If you need anything else from me, you know where to reach me."

Brent stood and shook her hand. "Thank you, Agent Zimmer. It's always a pleasure working with you."

Agent Zimmer smiled, turned, and left Brent and Agent Pan to sort out their next steps.

Chapter 33

Maricella was sitting in her bed playing with her favorite doll when she heard the door open. Haley came in quickly and closed the door behind her. She looked scared. Maricella was afraid something else had gone wrong.

"Mari, Lin left on some kind of business trip," whispered Haley. "Nurse Judy asked me to come and get you so she can talk to you."

Last night, Lin told Maricella and the others Judy would be staying with them. She said Judy was a nurse so they were to address her as such.

"Me? What does she want?"

"She's not going to tell me." Haley breathed a couple of times like she'd been running or something. "You have to remember not to tell Nurse Judy that we know about the harvesting. Do you understand?"

"Yeah, I guess."

Haley grabbed Maricella by her upper arms and shook her. Maricella had visions of her papá doing this very thing to her. It scared her so much she started to cry.

"Stop crying!" said Haley, still whispering in a rough manner. "You can't be saying 'I guess' when it comes to talking to Judy. If she finds out you know about the harvest, she'll tell Lin and then we'll all be in big trouble. You don't want us to be in trouble, do you?"

Maricella shook her head. "Let go. You're hurting me."

Haley let go of her and Maricella scooted off the bed and rubbed her arms to make them feel better. That's what Mamá would do after Papá squeezed her arms.

"I'm sorry, but this is very serious, Mari. No matter what she asks you, you can't let her know what we heard or ask her any questions about the harvesting."

Maricella started to get angry. Haley wasn't her boss. "I won't say anything! Where is Nurse Judy?"

"She's in Lin's office. You'd better hurry before she starts wondering why it took me so long to find you."

On her way down the hall, Maricella pulled up a sleeve and saw the red finger marks Haley had left. She hoped she wouldn't have to take off her shirt, because it would surely cause Nurse Judy to ask her what happened.

Maricella knocked on the door and Nurse Judy told her to come in. She was sitting on the pretty flowered couch along the wall.

"Hello, Maricella," said Nurse Judy. "Come sit here beside me, please."

For the first time, Maricella noticed Nurse Judy had very pretty blue eyes with flecks of green in them. Her red curls lay over the shoulders of her dark green sweater. Yesterday she wore her hair in a tight bun like Maricella's abuela wore sometimes. Today she looked younger and more friendly.

"So, my sweet girl, I've been told Nina wasn't very nice to you. Can you tell me what she did to hurt you?"

Maricella trembled at the thought of it. What if Nina came back? If Maricella got her into trouble, would she be meaner to her?

Nurse Judy placed her hand gently on Maricella's knee. "You look frightened, darling. There's no need to be scared. Miss Lin fired Nina and she will never come back here again. I promise you."

Looking up into the nurse's eyes, Maricella began to relax. Maybe Nurse Judy was a good person. However, Maricella told herself to only answer the questions and not talk about the harvest, just in case she'd tell Lin about their talk.

"Well, at first she just yelled at me a lot. She kept telling me I was bad and that's why my mamá wanted to get rid of me."

"She told you that? Oh, sweetie, I'm sure it isn't true. I hear you're a very good girl and *that's* why your mother gave you away. She couldn't take care of you any longer, so she gave you to someone who could provide you with everything you need."

"Will I ever get to see her again?" Maricella brightened at the prospect.

"I don't know. Probably not for a long time. We can discuss it later. Now, what I need to know is if Nina hurt you physically. Did she ever hit you?"

"She grabbed my arm sometimes and pulled it really hard. My shoulder would hurt for a long time. She never punched me or slapped me like she did John, but the day before she left, she dragged me down the stairs into the basement. Then she locked me in a really dirty closet."

"What was it like?"

"It smelled really bad, like somebody used the bathroom in there, and dark and scary. I couldn't see anything. I had a mattress to sit on. It was a really big closet, but I stayed on the edge of the mattress because I couldn't see."

"Lin said she didn't think you'd been in there very long."

"It seemed like a long time."

Judy smiled at Maricella and stroked her right cheek. "I'm sure it did. Nina should never have treated you so cruelly. Miss Lin made sure she won't be taking care of children ever again."

"That's good," said Maricella, sitting up a little straighter. "I don't think she likes kids."

"Have you been eating? You look a little too skinny to me."

Maricella thought about it. "When I first came here, I missed Mamá a lot, so I didn't eat very much. Then Jack and I became friends. He told me not eating wouldn't make them take me back, so I started eating. Jack is a really good cook. He said Daryl showed him how."

"Jack is a very nice young man. It's good he's looking out for you. Do you and Haley get along?"

"She's still misses her parents a lot, so sometimes she gets grumpy."

Nurse Judy took Maricella's chin in her hand and stared into her eyes. "She hasn't done anything to hurt you, has she?"

"Oh, no. Haley would never do that."

"Tomorrow, Dr. Sun will be here. He will be giving you a thorough examination to make sure you're healthy. Then very soon, he'll take you on a trip one day. How does that sound?"

Maricella wasn't sure what to say. It sounded exciting, but a little scary. "I think I'd like it."

"If you have no chores, you may go back to your room now."

Maricella felt good about talking to Nurse Judy, and now she would be going on a trip. She hoped Dr. Sun was as nice as Nurse Judy. She arrived at her room to find Haley still there.

"What did she have to say?" asked Haley.

"I think you're wrong about her. I liked her."

"Don't let her fool you with her sweet talk. What did she say?"

"Dr. Sun is coming tomorrow to look at me. Then I get to go on a trip with him soon."

"What?" yelled Haley, causing Maricella to jump.

"What's the matter?" asked Maricella. "He just wants to make sure I'm okay."

"This isn't good, Mari. We have to talk to Jack. We'll ask if we can help him with the chickens before lunch."

"Okay." Maricella's heart thumped at Haley's alarm. Why would seeing the doctor be bad?

"Come help me with the bathrooms so I can get them done faster." Haley turned to Maricella, gently taking her by the shoulders. "Don't worry. Jack will know what to do."

Chapter 34

"Here's the file we have on Dwayne Glover," said Detective Jackson. "Ambitious type. Smart. He had charm and used it to make friends."

"Did he ever inform on anybody?" asked Barnes. "Maybe somebody he snitched on decided to get revenge."

"Nah. Not sayin' he didn't play both ends against the middle sometimes, but he was definitely out for number one. I even heard he'd been talking to some disgruntled Hombres."

"Why were they disgruntled?" asked Samuels.

"Word on the street is neither gang wanted to get into the trafficking of little kids. We think the sickos who did want to may have gotten together. If any of the Blood found out he'd been talking to Hombres, he'd be as good as dead."

"Who's taken the Los Hombres lead on the outside since Hector Fuentes went to prison?" asked Barnes.

"Angel Valdez. Mean as they come. Probably why Fuentes picked him."

Barnes noticed the detective at the desk behind Jackson being a little too nosey for her taste. "Hey, you," she said pointing at him.

He looked behind him then pointed to himself. "Who, me?"

"You have anything to add to our conversation?" asked Barnes.

He stood up and came over to Detective Jackson's desk. "I heard Glover's name. I had run ins with him a few times."

"Detectives Barnes and Samuels, Homicide," said Jackson. "Detectives, this is Lewis Paxton."

"So I take it the two of you have been assigned to find out who killed Glover and Flores?"

"You take it right," said Barnes. "Do you have any insight as to who would want to murder Glover?"

"I guess I was just curious why Gangs isn't handling this since it's an obvious drive by," said Detective Paxton.

His response made the hairs on the back of Erica's neck stand on end. She wasn't sure why, but she felt instant distrust for this man.

"Murder is homicide, Detective Paxton," said Barnes. "It doesn't really matter who killed them. Besides, whoever did this killed one of ours and wounded another."

"What's your problem, Paxton?" asked Jackson. "With all the other crap we have on our plates, I'd think you'd be happy someone else gets this one."

"Flores *was* one of ours first," said Paxton. "How is Detective Kendall doing?"

"She's doing great," said Barnes. "Should be out of the hospital in a couple of days, but won't be back to work for a while."

Paxton nodded. He started to walk back to his desk then hesitated and turned back to them. "Did she see who shot her, or can she describe the vehicle?"

Erica raised her eyebrows and quickly glanced at Detective Samuels. "Why do you ask?"

"If we knew what type of vehicle or what the guy looked like, maybe one of us could figure out who might be involved. We've got a list of vehicles owned by gang affiliates."

"He's right," said Jackson. "If you get any kind of description, we might be able to narrow down your suspect list."

"Thanks for the offer," said Barnes. "Right now Chennelle's in shock and doesn't remember much, but the doc says it will improve with time."

Rising from her chair, she signaled for Samuels to do the same. Detective Jackson also stood and offered her his hand.

"Good to meet you, Detectives. Let me know if you need anything else. Flores was a good man. I want to find this S. O. B. as badly as you do."

"Thanks, Jackson," said Barnes.

Once alone on the elevator, Barnes turned to Samuels. "What did you think of Paxton?"

"I don't know. I guess I felt a little weird. He's got a look about him or something."

"I had similar feelings. As far as I'm concerned, we only work with Detective Jackson on this. Agreed?"

"Yeah. Him I trust."

"Okay. Now on to Angel Valdez."

Chapter 35

Maricella and Haley waited as Jack approached Nurse Judy. "Do you care if the girls go out to the chicken coop with me? I think they could use some fresh air."

"I think that's a great idea. Before you go out there, why don't you show Maricella how to build a snowman? No snowball fights though. Maricella is much younger than you and Haley and she could get hurt."

Jack agreed and told the girls to bundle up. They followed his orders and were out the door in minutes.

"Jack, like I told you," said Haley, "Mari had a long talk with Judy yesterday."

"Shush! Wait until we're out of earshot. Judy said to show Mari how to build a snowman, so we'll have plenty of time."

"I already know how to—"

Jack cut Maricella off. "She doesn't know that. Now be quiet until I tell you it's okay."

They walked far away from the house, almost to the woods where there was a large empty area of beautiful new snow. Maricella saw Jack start a ball of snow and roll it to make it bigger. She and Haley did likewise. When Jack's snowball was as big as a beach ball, he stopped.

"Now, tell me everything Judy said to you Mari," he said.

Maricella relayed everything she could remember. When she told him the doctor was coming to examine her, she noticed Jack close his eyes and put his hands on his hips.

"What's the matter, Jack?" she asked.

"I told you the doctor coming was bad," said Haley.

"Quit scaring her," snapped Jack. "She doesn't understand what's happening."

"I know," Haley retorted. "But this is really serious. I don't want her to get hurt any more than you do. We have to get her out of here."

"But it's too cold and snowy," whined Maricella. She didn't want to sound like a baby, but just because Jack told Haley not to scare her, didn't keep her from being scared. She couldn't understand how a doctor could hurt her. Weren't they supposed to make people feel better?

Jack came over to her and gently placed his hands on her shoulders. "I know it is, but Haley's right. This is very serious. I also know you're scared, but try not to let anybody know. Okay?"

"But why can't we ride on Daryl's horse so we can go away faster," asked Maricella.

"Because he's meaner than a snake. He'd buck us off in a second," said Jack. "If we took the other two, Mari could ride with me."

Maricella nodded. She wasn't sure how not to hide her fear from the others. She decided she'd avoid the adults as much as she could until Jack came up with a plan. Jack was smart. He'd make sure she didn't get hurt.

"Just because the doctor is coming, doesn't mean they're ready for her," said Jack. "He probably needs to get a blood sample to test. She has to match. We'll have to keep listening to see if Judy makes plans to transport her somewhere."

"What happens if we don't hear it and they take her before we can do anything?" asked Haley. "I think we should run now."

"It's not that simple," said Jack. "Daryl's going to be back tonight, so there will be two adults here guarding us. Then tomorrow, Dr. Sun will be here. We have to pick a day when it's just Judy again. We also need to watch the weather. If we can go during a time when it's not snowing and the north wind isn't blowing too much, we'll have a better chance."

"That's an awful lot of stuff we have to think about," said Haley. "You're making it too complicated."

"That's because it is complicated. I'm telling you, if Daryl is here, he'll hunt us down. He knows how to track animals in the woods, and the snow will make us easy targets." Jack sighed. "Haley, the man's been hunting most of his life. He'd bring Chaser with him, and they'd find us pretty quick."

"Okay, okay, we'll do it your way. Mari and I won't stand a chance going without you." Haley started rolling her snowball again. "We'd better get this snowman made in case Judy is watching."

By the time they were finished, Jack's ball of snow was huge. Haley's was almost as big, so it would go in the middle. Maricella waited as they hoisted it on top of the bigger snowball. She patted hers to pack the snow tightly as her snowball would be its head. Of course, Jack would have to place it on top, because she couldn't reach that high.

The three of them went to the edge of the woods to see if they could find two branches for the arms. There were a couple of low branches that Jack snapped off easily. They used a small twig for the nose.

"What are we going to use for its mouth and eyes?" asked Maricella. Her mind was set on making a great snowman now that she'd nearly forgotten the scary stuff.

"Over here," Jack said.

He showed them a small bush with some hard red berries on it. "Gather some of those holly berries for the mouth, but don't eat them. They're poisonous. I'll dig in the snow by that oak to see if I can find a couple of acorns for the eyes."

Once they'd gathered everything, Jack finished the snowman's face. At home, Maricella used rocks for the eyes and mouth, but the red berries looked much better. Red, like a real mouth. Rocks weren't always the same size either, but the acorns were and brown like her eyes.

They were all admiring their handiwork when Jack began to speak. "Here's what we need to do. We need to pack some stuff ahead of time. It can't be a lot, but it won't matter because we won't be taking baths until we find someone who will help us."

"How can we do it without Judy finding out?" asked Haley.

He looked at Haley. "When you do laundry and go to put it in our drawers, slip a couple pairs of socks and underwear of yours and Mari's into my things. I'll take care of the packing."

"Won't she or Daryl find this stuff?" asked Haley.

"I'll put our packs in the chicken coop. Judy doesn't go in there, and Daryl leaves the egg gathering and feeding to me. He won't go in there unless there's a problem. I've got a good hiding spot." He paused. "I'll slip some food in as I go along, too. Some beef jerky, canned stuff, you know, things that don't spoil. It won't be hard."

"I guess you know what you're doing," said Haley.

Maricella wasn't sure Haley really believed it. However, *she* did. Whatever Jack said would be the truth. She trusted him.

"Okay, girls. You go on back to the house while I clean out the coop. If she asks why you didn't go with me, tell her I thought Mari was getting too wet and cold. I'll be back at the house in a few minutes."

Maricella trotted along behind Haley as fast as she could. Even going her fastest, she was several feet behind the other girl The thought of trying to run away in snow this deep seemed impossible. She hoped the horses could walk okay in it. Jack was right. They needed to wait. In the meantime, she'd do what Abuela Elena always told her to do—she would pray.

Chapter 36

The ringing of his cell phone interrupted Brent's conversation with Agent Pan. "Freeman," he answered.

"It's Natalie. I wanted to tell you I'm going to be late tonight, so you should grab some dinner."

"That's okay. Agent Pan and I have some more things to discuss."

"I see," she said.

Natalie's silent departure wasn't a good sign. No, *okay I'll see you later,* or *are you sure you're feeling up to working so late?* Just, *I see.*

"I'll see you at home then," he said as cheerfully as he could muster.

"Yes. I'm not sure how late I'll be."

"Okay, I'll probably beat you home then. Love you."

"Goodbye," she said before disconnecting.

He placed the phone back in his pocket and rubbed his eyes.

"Are you sure you're up to this, Detective?" asked Agent Pan.

"I'm fine," he lied. He really wanted another Vicodin. "Wish my sister hadn't gone back to Kokomo. Then I'd have a dinner companion."

"It's nearly five-thirty. Would you like to have some dinner with me? There's a lovely restaurant in my hotel, and it's just around the block. We could talk business while we eat. You'll get home sooner."

Brent could hardly pass it up. The day *had* made him weary. No point in pushing it to the point of exhaustion. The doctor might revoke his work privileges. He agreed and offered to drive her over. Even though the hotel was close by, the wind blew much too coldly today for a walk.

The maître-d seated them with menus and took their drink orders. When Brent requested iced tea and Nuwa asked for water with lemon, he gave them a funny look. Nevertheless, Brent refused to mix his pain meds with anything that might get him a DUI, or worse.

"This whole thing with the gang involvement is really complicating things, isn't it?" said Agent Pan. "Of course, when you put it into perspective, these child traffickers are simply gangs of older, more sophisticated thugs."

"I thought most human trafficking involved teens, either for prostitution or slavery," said Brent. "Kidnapping a five-year-old. It doesn't make sense."

"Organ harvesting is big business as is anything where desperate people are found."

"So I guess the recipients don't care how they get the organs as long as *their* child is saved." Brent's heart began to thump at the notion of these people taking this little girl to carve up into pieces.

"They don't ask, because they don't want to know," said Pan. "That's why it's important to get the word out to the public. Maybe then they won't be able to ignore the fact that healthy children are being slaughtered and might think twice before going this route."

"How do they manage to get these organs into a system that's so carefully regulated?"

"Unfortunately, every system can be broken," said Agent Pan. "The motivator here is greed. These unscrupulous physicians, nurses, and other health professionals value money over life. Donor wait lists are long. They find parents who are desperately trying to find a donor so their child won't die. Again, the parents don't question what the doctor is doing and will travel anywhere for the surgery. Their only focus is on saving their child's life."

"It's so hard to believe human trafficking has become so prevalent in this country," said Brent.

"Oh, Sergeant Freeman, think about it. Human trafficking has been around for centuries. Let's not forget the buying and selling of human slaves in this country, which began before the Revolutionary War. Prostitution of young girls has been around for many years as well. Anytime one sells a human being as property, it's human trafficking."

Brent picked up his menu. Although he understood the point Pan made, the thought of buying and selling children made it even more horrendous.

After a waiter brought their drinks and took their dinner order, Agent Pan pulled out her electronic notepad. She read off all of the facts they had thus far. After a brief pause, she turned the notepad around so Brent could see it.

"This is who I suspect is behind this," said Pan. "Han Wu. He's based in China, but Intelligence tells us he's been branching out to the U.S. For some reason, he's chosen the Midwest as his primary hunting grounds."

"Maybe he thinks we're too stupid to catch on," said Brent. "When people from out of state visit, they're always shocked to find Indianapolis a growing, thriving city. I get tired of meeting with cops from huge cities who ask me how it is in India-*nap*-olis. Of course, I'm not too crazy about the murder rate increasing, but this is a great city."

"I've noticed." Agent Pan paused and smiled at him, her big

brown eyes teasing him. "You're very passionate about your city and about this case. I like that in a cop."

"Thanks, I think." Brent smiled and could feel the blood rushing to his face. He hoped the dim lighting didn't reveal the flush of his cheeks.

"You're welcome. Now, back to Han Wu. I suspect he's chosen the Midwest because his people don't have to drive very far to find rural areas. Agent Zimmer agrees. Southern Indiana, Kentucky, and Tennessee have lots of areas suited for this."

"I see your point. Does Intelligence have any clue as to where we should start?"

"We're looking for red flags from banks when it comes to people making large deposits. Of course, we can't be sure they're using local banks, but sometimes traffickers do pick people who aren't particularly...*intelligent* or wealthy, because they are most vulnerable to the temptation. These assistants don't ask what's being done with the children, they simply collect the cash."

"So, they didn't expect our murder victim, Lucia Colon, to be awake. The kidnappers didn't go in intending to kill her?"

"No, although we did find Nina Clemente had an arrest record for assault from a few years back. In addition, she lived in the same general area as your victim. Maybe she killed Lucia Colon because she knew Lucia would recognize her. Perhaps she had to kill her because Mrs. Colon let her in. If you recall, your CSI told us they found no forced entry."

Brent considered this as the waiter placed their dinners in front of them. It made sense. "I think we should have Carlos Colon come in again so we can question him. If Clemente knew his wife, he should know."

"Great idea. Now let's stop all this shop talk and dig into these fabulous steaks."

Nuwa Pan smiled at him again, and for the first time, he

noticed her beauty. Her smile lit up her face. Dark silky hair lay across her shoulders and shimmered in the candle light, which reflected in her deep brown eyes. He blinked, shook his head, and picked up his knife and fork. He had to stop this appraisal. Cutting off a piece of meat, he chewed it slowly while wondering if this was how Natalie saw Agent Pan, potentially triggering her jealous reaction.

During dinner they chatted about family, friends, and how they got started in their respective careers. Brent soon learned that Nuwa's paternal grandparents emigrated from China fifty years ago and settled in Chicago's Chinatown. That was where her father met her mother, and they still lived there running a gift shop. She was their only daughter, and she had four brothers—much the same situation as his what with him being the only son with three sisters.

When they parted and Brent started his car, he looked at the clock and realized it was after nine o'clock. He'd been having such a pleasant conversation, he'd lost track of time. His only hope for a good night's sleep now would hinge on getting home before Natalie did or taking an extra Vicodin.

Chapter 37

Erica approached Brent's desk with an air of caution. He'd shown up at her door last night at eleven asking her and Ben if he could stay in their guest room. She had decided to give him a break and forego any interrogation since she assumed she knew why he showed up there. The more she got to know Natalie Ralston, the less she liked her.

"Hey, boss." She tried to keep it light, because he looked like crap. "You sure got up early. We had planned to make you a fine breakfast, but found you gone."

"I really don't want to talk about it, Barnes," he said.

"No need." Erica placed a key on his desk. "You can stay with us as long as you want. Ben and I can test out what it's like to have a child."

Brent rolled his eyes and gave her a cute little smirk. "Can it, Barnes."

"I knew I could get you to smile. Now, on to business. Samuels and I talked to Jackson in Gangs and found out Angel Valdez is handling things since Fuentes went to prison. He's here and waiting for me to interview him in two. Did you want to join Samuels in the observation room?"

"I think I'll sit this one out," he said, looking down and shuffling some papers. "Thanks for taking over training Detective Samuels."

"Not a problem. She's bright and listens. I think she's going to be great." Erica paused and peered at the dark circles under Brent's eyes. How could Natalie treat him so badly, especially when he'd only been out of the hospital a few days? He needed to get away from her.

Erica decided not to say anything further. She peeked into the observation room to let Samuels know she'd be going in. There he sat, leaning back in his chair with the uncooperative smugness these gang thugs portrayed.

"Good morning, Mr. Valdez. I'm Detective Barnes. Thanks for coming in today."

He looked her up and down as she took her seat across the table from him. "Man, the P.D. sure is hiring a lot of pretty detectives these days. First the lady detective puts me in here and now you. Oh, and the best lookin' one, no offense, is the one who got shot. She shoulda been making music videos. She's one fine woman."

"How do you know what Detective Kendall looks like?"

"I watch the news. They been showing pictures of her and Detective Flores ever since it happened."

Erica watched him closely to see if he was enjoying their fate or simply trying to rattle her. She decided to get right to it.

"About that, do you know of anyone who'd want to take out Dwayne Glover?"

"I think you got a long list there, Detective." Valdez sat forward, putting his elbows on the table. "You see, when you're a snitch, nobody likes you. Seems to me he was playin' too many ends against the middle, if you know what I mean."

"Humor me. Pretend I'm stupid and explain it to me."

"He's a Blood, so that makes him stink, but when you go against your own...not cool. From what I hear, he wanted to get into something and his *Brothers* didn't. When it didn't work, he was tryin' to get some Hombres interested. Like we'd do business with a Blood."

"Any idea what type of business he wanted to start?"

"Sellin' kids."

Valdez seemed to be giving up this information too easily. Erica needed to approach the rest of this conversation cautiously.

"So he wanted to get into human trafficking, specifically kids. That could be age one day to seventeen. What do you mean by kids?"

"I'm talkin' zero to twelve."

Erica hoped her face didn't show the shock she felt at this moment. She had to get her brain to cooperate and get as much out of Valdez as possible.

"That's pretty young."

"Los Hombres doesn't sell kids, and if they did, they wouldn't sell one of their own."

Obviously, he referred to Maricella Colon. Erica sat back in her chair appraising Valdez's body language. He still leaned forward and actually looked serious when talking about the kids. She needed to determine if he was truly concerned for the children or if he was trying to steer her away from his involvement with trafficking.

"So who does? Are there any rumors about who is trying to recruit in this area?"

Valdez sat back in the chair again, slinging one arm over the back of it. Again, he took on a smug persona. "Maybe I heard something about China."

"That it?" asked Barnes. She couldn't believe he'd clam up now.

"Yeah, may I go now, Detective?"

"I'll get your escort." She stood and waited for Samuels to come around to let her out.

Just as the door started to open, Valdez said, "You might want to clean up your own house, pretty lady."

Chapter 38

Maricella left Haley and Jack in the kitchen cleaning up the breakfast dishes. Dr. Sun had arrived and waited for her in Lin's office. Her heart pounded as she thought about him using a needle to take her blood. She hated needles. What else would he do to her? Was he as nice as Nurse Judy?

Hearing voices as she approached the office door, Maricella stopped and listened.

"The child appears to be in very good health," said Nurse Judy. "I don't think Nina had time to do any real damage."

"That's good," said Dr. Sun. "We have customers waiting for items such as the liver, heart, and kidney. I need to do the blood tests as soon as possible before someone else beats us to it."

"I understand. I just wish…."

"You're not becoming attached to the girl, are you?" he asked.

Nurse Judy hesitated. "No, of course not. It wouldn't be wise."

"No, indeed," said the doctor. "Where is she? I don't have all day."

Maricella heard someone walking towards the door. She didn't want them to know she was listening, so she hurried back to the end of the hallway and pretended she'd just arrived.

"Oh, there you are," said Nurse Judy. "Come along, dear. The doctor is waiting."

Maricella hurried along the hallway, her face getting hot and her stomach churning. She hoped she wouldn't lose her bacon all over the doctor's shoes.

"Ah, there she is," said Dr. Sun. He sat down in a chair. "Come here so I can have a look at you."

Usually when she went to the doctor, Maricella would sit on this big bed-like thing. They didn't have one of those here, so she stood in front of the doctor while he checked her ears, used his listening thing to hear her heart, and used a temperature thing they stick in people's ears.

"So far, you appear to be in excellent health." The doctor stood up, picked Maricella up, and sat her on the chair. "Now, Nurse Judy will take some blood out of your arm. I won't lie to you; it will hurt a little. But, you must be very brave and sit very still until she is finished. Okay?"

Maricella nodded. What she wanted to do was scream, or cry, or run. If she did any of those things, they'd catch her and the doctor would hold her down. This scared her so much, she couldn't move if she tried.

The rubber band pinched her skin and she looked away. Nurse Judy had her squeeze a soft ball and then smacked her arm a few times. She used a smelly cold thing to wipe Maricella's arm.

"Sit very still, Maricella," said Nurse Judy. "You're going to feel a little stick now."

Maricella couldn't help it; she flinched a little, but not enough to move her arm. Tears streamed down her face as she continued to look away. Maybe it wouldn't hurt so bad if she kept looking at the pretty red dragon on Lin's desk.

The next thing she knew, Nurse Judy had put a piece of cotton on the spot where the needle had been and wrapped a bandage over it. Then she pulled Maricella's sleeve back down over her arm.

"There, that wasn't so bad, was it?"

Maricella wiped the tears from her face and smiled at Nurse Judy. It really wasn't as bad as she'd expected. "Can I go now?" she asked.

"I just have one more thing to do," said Dr. Sun. "Hopefully it won't tickle."

He had her get out of the chair and told her to face him. He put one hand on her shoulder and one on her belly. He started pushing in different spots. It really felt weird, but she remembered her doctor doing this, too. Nobody ever told her why. Then he turned her around and pushed on her back a few times.

"All right, Maricella. You may go now," he said.

She hurried from the room and back to the kitchen. Haley and Jack turned as she entered. She started to speak, but Jack put his finger to his lips.

"Not yet," he said. "We're done with the dishes, so it's time to feed the chickens."

Haley helped Maricella into her coat and boots. Once ready, Jack called down the hall to tell Nurse Judy where they were going.

As soon as they entered the chicken coop, Jack rounded on her. "What did they say? What did they do to you?"

Maricella told them everything from the doctor having those customers waiting to the examination. She didn't like the way Jack looked when she finished.

"They'll probably have those blood tests back in a few days," said Jack as he paced. He frowned at Haley. "If she's a match, they'll take her right away, immediately."

"So what are we going to do?" asked Haley.

"Daryl is supposed to leave tomorrow to go to his parents'

house in Lexington. He'll take Chaser with him. He loves that hound more than a real kid. The point is, he's not supposed to be back until the day after Christmas."

"Tomorrow is Christmas Eve," said Haley, her face reddening. "We've got to get her out of here."

"I know, I know," he said. "Lexington is two hours away. If we leave after Judy goes to sleep, we'll have at least an eight hour lead before she calls Daryl."

"But what about Santa?" asked Maricella.

Haley and Jack turned and looked at her real funny. Then they glanced at one another and Haley shook her head. Jack went to Maricella and crouched in front of her, taking her hands.

"This year, Mari, I'm your Santa Claus."

Chapter 39

"He told me to 'clean my own house,'" said Barnes. "Sarge, I think he's confirming we have a dirty cop among us."

Brent ran his fingers through his hair and leaned back in his chair. "That's all we need. Geez, aren't things complicated enough without throwing something else in the mix?"

A new headache started causing his temples to throb. He reached in his pocket for a Vicodin, and then he saw Natalie striding toward his desk, her eyes blazing.

"So, where did you go last night?" said Natalie. She glanced down at his desk. "And whose key is this?"

"He stayed at my place and it's a key to my house," said Barnes. "He's welcome to stay with Ben and I as long as necessary."

Brent couldn't believe Natalie would come to his office and embarrass him in front of his colleagues. He could feel everyone's eyes on him now. Afraid Barnes would go off on Natalie at any second, he turned to her and told her to take her partner out for some lunch and run her new theory past Samuels. Barnes took the hint but glared at Natalie as she and Samuels left the area.

"Natalie, this is where I work. My boss is just over there in his office. This kind of behavior looks bad for you as well as for me. If you want to talk, I suggest we go to dinner tonight and discuss where this relationship is heading."

Natalie's eyes narrowed to snake-like slits then she slammed a file on his desk. "Here are the copies of my notes from the Fuentes case. My boss told me you needed them."

"Good morning, Sergeant Freeman."

Agent Pan stood behind Natalie now. Natalie closed her eyes and took a deep breath in what Brent could only guess was her way of getting hold of herself. "I know you took most of my Vicodin," she whispered. Then she turned around stiffly. "Good morning, Agent Pan. He's all yours."

She stomped away like a spoiled child. Brent could feel his embarrassment flush his cheeks. He turned in time to see Detective Osaka shift his attention back to his computer.

"Sorry about her," he said to Agent Pan.

"Not a problem for me. I'm just sorry she's being so…difficult."

Leave it to Agent Pan to put a good spin on things. Sure Barnes had a much different word for Natalie, he started to think about the fact this relationship wasn't working out. Now he needed to decide how to get out of it.

"You told me you planned to take a few steps back today and see if you could find something from an old case," said Pan. "Were you able to do that?"

"I'm hoping to find something in this file. It's the case Natalie prosecuted that put Hector Fuentes away. Fuentes had a sister who fell for one of the Blood Brothers. Fuentes murdered him and I investigated that case. I'm hoping this file will contain something they didn't need for trial, but which might help us with our case."

"Well, then, it sounds like we need to get to work. Give me half and we'll go through it together."

Agent Pan took a seat at Kendall's vacant desk and started going through her half. Brent found it difficult to concentrate after his most recent encounter with Natalie. He'd promised his mother he and Natalie would come to Kokomo to share Christmas with her. Now what? Should he call and tell her he wasn't feeling well? He hated disappointing her, but it would be so embarrassing to have his two older sisters harass him about Natalie's absence. He could hear them now, raving about how many failed relationships he'd had, how he'd never find the right one, et cetera. Of course, his twin, Brenda, would support him and try to fend off the others. He felt it might be better to give his mother a little disappointment rather than totally ruining her Christmas.

"I'm not sure of the significance, but I just found a little note here about Carlos Colon and his cousin, *Nina Clemente*," said Agent Pan, bringing Brent out of his thoughts with a jolt.

"Colon and Clemente are cousins?"

"That's what it says here. You questioned her about Fuentes's whereabouts at the time of the murder. Fuentes disposed of his clothes in the garbage behind a McDonalds. Clemente worked at that same McDonalds."

"I'd forgotten about her. She said she hadn't seen him that night. Wonder if she and Carlos Colon were close, because it doesn't make sense she would be involved in murdering his wife or taking his daughter, unless…."

"Unless he was in on it," said Pan, rising and coming over to Brent's desk. She started talking excitedly. "You said when Detective Mayhew interviewed him, he appeared to be distraught about his daughter going missing."

"Samuels and I watched. He looked genuinely shocked about his wife's death and became very agitated about the girl."

"What if he hired his cousin to snatch the child for him and she double-crossed him?" she asked, her eyes sparkling with enthusiasm.

"Looks like it's time for us to have another chat with Carlos Colon."

Chapter 40

Samuels and Barnes sat down at the table with their lunch. Anne still felt embarrassed for Sergeant Freeman. She would die if somebody came into her office and started yelling at her the way Natalie just yelled at the sergeant.

"She's getting on my last nerve," said Barnes. "Brent Freeman is a great guy. I'm sure he treats her like a queen. Yet she has the nerve to come in and humiliate him in front of his department. She's the one who told him to find another place to sleep last night."

"Really?" Anne's sympathy for the sergeant grew by the minute.

"Sorry. Please don't repeat that. There's enough freakin' gossip around here. When you've partnered with him more than once, you'll see what I mean about him."

Anne nodded. "I already know what you mean. He's always polite and really patient with me. I've seen how he treats everybody. He's fair and has a good sense of humor, and...."

"Whoa there, girl. Let's not get too carried away. If he catches wind of all this praise, it might go to his fat head."

"It's fun to watch the two of you banter back and forth," said Anne. "It keeps things light. Considering some of the horror we have to deal with, a little humor goes a long way."

"Even if it's sick humor?"

Anne smiled at her and then dug into her chicken salad. Chewing a particularly large chunk of chicken, she couldn't warn Barnes that Detective Paxton was coming up behind her.

"Detectives," he said. "Did you get a chance to talk to Angel Valdez yet?"

"Yeah, I talked to him this morning," said Barnes.

"He say anything that might help you?" asked Paxton.

"Same old thing…wasn't his crew."

The look on Barnes's face told Anne to keep the interview between them. This guy wasn't somebody she or Barnes trusted. Anne suspected he could feel their disdain.

"That's too bad," said Paxton. "If I can help in any way, just let me know. Got to get back to work."

Barnes gave him a quick nod then watched him leave the cafeteria. Anne hoped she'd never do anything to earn that look.

"You still don't trust him, do you?" asked Anne.

"Nope." Barnes took a small bite of her sandwich, chewing slowly and washing it down with her tea. "Samuels, I don't want you talking to anybody about this case but me, Freeman, and Pan. If we understood Valdez right, we don't have any idea who to trust."

"Of course, I caught your signal," said Anne. She saw movement behind Barnes again. "Looks like more company. At least this time he's welcome."

Barnes peered over her shoulder as Sergeant Freeman approached.

"Good, you're here," said Freeman.

"You sent me to lunch, didn't you?" Barnes always had to give the sergeant a hard time.

"Yes…but you could have gone down the street or something," said Freeman. "Listen to this. Pan and I just discovered Nina Clemente and Carlos Colon are cousins."

"Seriously?" Barnes dropped her sandwich and turned his way. "So are we back to Colon arranging the kidnapping?"

"I sent a squad to pick him up and bring him here. Could just be a coincidence. Could be he ticked her off and she decided to double-cross him."

"He seemed so upset when Detective Mayhew interviewed him," said Anne. Her heart rate went up a little as they stared at her. "What if Mr. Colon asked his cousin to kidnap the girl, but he didn't want his wife killed? Maybe that's why he went off the deep end."

"Agent Pan and I were discussing that very thing," said the sergeant.

"As a mother, I think taking Maricella would be the best way for him to get back at his wife for having him incarcerated. It would have driven her crazy," said Anne. "I bet he knows about Ms. Clemente's involvement in the trafficking. When he didn't hear from her right away, he knew he'd been tricked and she'd sold Maricella instead of hiding her for him."

"Dang, Sarge. You didn't ruin her after all," said Barnes, clapping him on the shoulder.

Anne saw her boss wince in pain, but didn't think Barnes was paying attention. On her end, however, this confirmation of her aptitude felt great.

"Do you want to help me with the interview?" asked Freeman.

Anne realized he was asking her and she jumped on it. "You bet."

Brent stood up. "You two stick around then. He should be here by two." He left them to their lunch.

"Wow, look at you," said Barnes. "Good police work, Detective."

"Thanks." Anne suddenly experienced some panic. "Could you...would you go over a few questions with me. You know...help me practice a little."

Barnes grinned at her and picked up her sandwich. "Finish up and we'll get on it."

Chapter 41

Chennelle settled down in her bed to take a nap. Her lunch hadn't settled well, so Trevon had gone down to the cafeteria to see if he could get her some saltine crackers. She closed her eyes, trying to remember the car. It was black and large, but what make? Frustration caused her to open her eyes in time to see someone in scrubs closing her door.

"Who are you?" she asked. The fact he wore a surgical mask and gloves put her on high alert. She sat up and reached for her buzzer.

He immediately lunged for her. She could see the hypodermic needle in his right hand as he grabbed her with his left. An excruciating pain shot through her shoulder, but she had to keep fighting or die. She lashed out, scratching his neck with her fingernails. Startled, he dropped the needle and punched her in the jaw.

Reeling from the impact, Chennelle pressed the alert button. She noticed he'd recovered the syringe. With her head spinning, she groped at his face trying to pull off his mask. He slammed his hand into her chest and pushed her down flat on her back as she screamed in pain.

The door flew open, banging against the wall, and a nurse rushed in. The scene in the room stopped her dead in her tracks, "What are you doing?" she called out in surprise. Reality hit her as the masked man turned to glare at her. "Somebody call Security!" she shouted.

The man again dropped the needle as he slammed into the nurse, knocking her down. Trevon arrived at the door just as the intruder went flying through it.

"What the...," Trevon said, glancing down in confusion. He helped the stunned nurse to her feet. She grabbed his sleeve with one hand, and with the other, pointed towards the door.

"He tried to kill her," she said, her voice trembling with shock. Trevon immediately ran out of the room in pursuit.

Chennelle writhed in pain. Blood spilled from the wound in her shoulder. Regaining control of both her emotions and the situation, the nurse yelled for personnel to call the resident. She then grabbed a dressing kit from the bedside cabinet, quickly donned gloves, and placed a sterile pad over Chennelle's wound.

"Try to relax, Detective. We may have to go back into surgery to repair what he's done to you."

"He had a syringe full of something."

"I know, dear, but he dropped it. The police will be here soon and they'll have it analyzed. I got here before he could inject you, so that's a plus."

The nurse was being so kind and gentle. She pulled down Chennelle's bloody gown as she continued applying pressure to the wound.

Having a hard time breathing, Chennelle knew she had to make sure someone knew about the scratch. "Tell the police...I scratched him. Forensics...collect the stuff...under my nails."

Suddenly her world turned chaotic. She heard the click-clack of a gurney being pushed into the room. Around her, people spoke tersely in worried voices. Most of all, she sensed hands...lots of hands. And then Chennelle felt herself lifted, her body seeming to fold in on itself as she was pulled onto the cart and hurriedly wheeled away.

She felt dizzier now, like she would pass out at any moment.

"Is she okay," she heard him say. "Chennelle, baby. It's going to be okay. They're going to fix you up."

Every slightest bump brought on a new wave of pain. Someone continued to put pressure on her wound. Bright lights overhead made her close her eyes. "The guy was white," she mumbled, and then everything went dark.

Chapter 42

Anne, Detective Barnes, and Sergeant Freeman were getting ready to start the Colon interrogation when Freeman's desk phone rang. Anne and Barnes stopped and waited for him.

"Are you serious?" he said. "Is she okay?"

From the look on his face and the tone in his voice, Anne knew this phone call could not be good. She watched him as he began to pace and push his fingers through his hair.

"Has CSI been notified?" He paused, nodding as if the caller could see him. "Try to stay calm, Trevon. I'll be there in a few minutes." He slammed down the receiver.

"Has something happened to Chennelle?" asked Barnes. Her usual banter and good humor had disappeared.

"Yes. Apparently, someone tried to kill her."

Anne's mouth dropped open and her heart skipped a beat. She glanced at Barnes and wondered if she felt the same since she had nothing to say.

"Trevon said the nurse heard Kendall screaming and ran into the room. She found someone standing over Chennelle holding a syringe. She said he's a white male about six-foot one, dressed in scrubs, mask, and gloves. Kendall told her she'd scratched this guy and to make sure we collect any evidence left under her fingernails. Always the great detective."

"Holy crap," said Barnes at last.

"The intruder busted open her wound, so she's in surgery," he said, then slammed his hands on his desk. "They'd planned to release her today."

"So what can we do?" asked Barnes.

"I've got to get down there. You two are on your own now with Colon," he said. "Samuels, you'll still be lead on this interrogation, but I want Barnes in there with you. These types always know when they've got a rookie."

"Yes, Sergeant," said Anne. She had been relying on him to be in there with her, but having Barnes by her side would definitely keep her on track.

"She's going to do great," said Barnes. "We've been practicing her technique. I think you'll find her to be pretty tough."

"I'm sure she is," said Freeman, giving Anne an approving grin. "I've got to get down to the hospital. Join me there when you're done with the interview."

He didn't wait for a confirmation. Grabbing his coat, he hurried toward the elevator while Anne and Erica walked towards Interrogation Room Three.

Anne took a deep breath, looked up at Barnes, and put her hand on the doorknob. "Well, here goes."

They entered the room and, as with many of their interviews of late, Carlos Colon sat in the stereotypical gangster's defiant manner. Anne smiled through her fear and introduced herself and Barnes to Colon before taking a seat.

"We discovered something interesting today," Anne began.

"Zat right?"

"Seems you have, or should I say had, a cousin by the name Nina Clemente."

Colon's face hardened, Anne's first clue of his anger toward his cousin.

"Were the two of you close?" she asked as Barnes scribbled notes.

"Not really," he answered.

"From what we hear, you two were really tight," said Anne. She hadn't heard this, but hoped it would prod him a little.

"Well, you know what they say about rumors."

"What would you say if I told you we have witnesses who swear you and Nina Clemente spent a lot of time together?" If this didn't work, she'd have to pull out the guilt card.

"I'd say they was lyin'. Ya know, you cops should quit hasslin' me and find my kid. She's been gone for over a week now."

Anne could see his demeanor change when he talked about Maricella. He truly didn't know where they had taken her. "Okay. So if you weren't close like we heard, could she have been upset with you for some reason? Would she take Maricella to get back at you?"

"Look, I don't know why you're askin' me about Nina. The big fat slob never worked a day in her life. She had three kids and DCFS took every one of them away from her. I don't think she liked kids much."

"Indulge me for a moment, Mr. Colon," said Anne. "Evidence is mounting that your cousin participated in a human trafficking organization. In a sense she *was* working, but not for the good guys. This particular organization deals in trafficking children. Do you know what they do with these children?"

Carlos started shifting in his seat, his jaw set ready to explode. Confident he knew the danger his daughter faced, Anne had to start playing the guilt card now.

"They sell them to the highest bidder. Usually the older ones are prepped for prostitution. Do you know what they do to five-year-olds?"

He placed his elbow on the table and rested his head on his fist. She had him now. All she had to do was give him the gory details.

"They cut them up, Mr. Colon."

He dropped his fist to the table and fear took the place of defiance. Swallowing hard, he looked away from her. Anne could practically hear the gears running in his head. She had to keep at him until he broke.

"That's right, Carlos. They sell their internal organs on the black market to desperate parents. They take lives to *save* others. Do you think that's a noble cause? One life to save three or four? Is this why you let Nina take her?"

"I didn't let Nina take her to be slaughtered! She was just supposed to hide her for me."

Carlos Colon burst into tears, slamming his fists on the table. Anne leaned back in her chair to give him a moment and noticed Barnes do the same. A moment was all she could give him, though, because she didn't want him composing himself to the point of clamming up again.

"You sanctioned the kidnapping, but she double-crossed you," said Anne.

"Yes, yes." He howled like a wounded animal before speaking again. "Lucia wouldn't let me see her. She said she was going to get full custody and I'd only have supervised visits. I wanted to teach her a lesson. Nobody was supposed to get hurt."

Now Anne needed to change her tactics. "You love Maricella, don't you?"

Colon nodded and turned his face to the ceiling. She wondered if he was praying, which would be a great idea right about now.

"If you love her, you have to help us find her before it's too late," she said. "Do you have any idea who Nina hung out with, or did she mention where they might hide her?"

Colon shook his head and wiped his nose on his sleeve. "She was supposed to call me to tell me where they took Maricella. She knew if I found out she had a hand in killing Lucia, I'd be coming after her. I thought she was waiting for me to cool off, but then someone took her out."

"So she had an accomplice. In your conversations with her prior to the kidnapping, you didn't meet this partner or get a name. You expect us to believe that, Carlos?"

Anne let him think this over. Barnes tapped her on the arm and showed her a notation in her notebook which said, *Great job— you're a natural.* Anne gave her a quick grin and then put her serious face back on for Colon.

"There was this white dude," he began. "His name started with a D. Darwin...David...no, Daryl. It was Daryl."

Excited about this break, Anne sat forward and caught his eye. "Did you get a last name?"

Colon shook his head. "Nah, but I remember what he looked like. Scrawny, dark hair, beard he hadn't trimmed for a long time. You got one of those artists I can talk to?"

Barnes handed her notebook to Anne. "I'll go arrange it," she said before leaving the room.

"Is there anything else about this man, or did you hear any other conversations you didn't think important? You might have heard or seen something that didn't seem relevant at the time."

"This guy had an accent. You know, like somebody down south." He paused, eyes wondering around the room. Then he sat up straighter, face brightening with discovery. "Kentucky. I saw a map on her table from Kentucky."

"That's very helpful," said Anne. Her body flushed with

enthusiasm over the best lead they had thus far. "I'm going to see if the sketch artist is on the way."

She exited the room, nearly running over Barnes. "He said this Daryl had a southern accent. He also saw a map of Kentucky on Nina Clemente's table."

"That's great," said Barnes. "Wait until Freeman hears this. He needs some good news right about now."

"I didn't tell him he'd be going to jail for violating his parole by conspiring to kidnap his daughter."

"Well, if he doesn't know it, he's dumber than I thought. Let's get his paperwork done. The FBI will want to do the arrest on the conspiracy charge since this one is a federal offense. He can sit in a holding cell until then."

In all her glee, Anne had almost forgotten about the attack on Chennelle Kendall. "Oh my gosh. We need to get over to the hospital."

"Don't worry," said Barnes. "The sarge has everything under control. He'd call us if there was any word."

Anne nodded, but couldn't help worrying.

Chapter 43

Haley walked down the hallway quietly. She'd been doing this ever since they started listening for clues about Maricella. Hearing Nurse Judy talking to someone on the phone in Lin's office, Haley crept up next to the door to listen.

"You have a preliminary match already?" asked Judy. "I understand that blood type is sufficient in most cases, but I thought you'd be doing some sort of cross matching to be sure."

There was a short pause before she continued. "So you think moving her on Christmas day is best."

Her heart quickened as Haley heard this; she knew they spoke of Maricella. There wasn't any snow in the forecast today. Maybe they could leave tonight.

"I'll have her ready by noon on Christmas. Thank you, doctor."

After hearing Nurse Judy ended the conversation, Haley crept back towards the kitchen to find Jack preparing dinner. She whispered all she'd heard to him.

Jack frowned at her. "I can't believe they got those test results back so fast. I thought it would be at least a week."

"Well, it sounded like he didn't do all the testing yet. Maybe this bunch of thieves don't care about it."

"Right... Then we need to get ready to go. It's not going to be as cold tonight as it has been, but it will be plenty cold enough.

You need to make sure Maricella has lots of warm clothes, especially socks and gloves. Someone her size can get frostbite a lot quicker than you or me."

"When are we going to leave?" she asked. Her anxiety had her stomach tied up in knots.

"Daryl is leaving tonight for Lexington. We have to give him at least a four-hour lead. Then we have to be sure Judy is good and asleep." Jack paused for a moment and then opened one of the cabinets. "Yes," he said.

"What is it?" asked Haley.

"We've got some Valerian root extract left."

"What's that?"

"It's a plant. One of the women who used to be here to take care of us a few years ago used it as a tea to put her to sleep. She had a really hard time falling asleep sometimes and knew a lot about herbs and how they worked. I'll put more than the normal amount in Judy's tea this evening and she'll sleep all night."

"Are you sure?" Haley didn't know how tea would knock somebody out all night.

"Yes, I'm sure. This way she won't know we're missing until we've been gone for hours. By the time she gets Daryl to drive back here, we'll be long gone. We may even find somebody who'll help us by then."

This was exactly what Haley wanted to hear. She'd be free to go home, maybe even be able to spend Christmas with her family. "Okay. You finish dinner and I'll go find Mari. This is going to work."

Chapter 44

Brent paced back and forth, occasionally combing his fingers through his brown curls. Doing this felt comforting to him in this stressful time. He couldn't lose another detective, especially not Chennelle. Besides being a great detective, she was a fantastic person.

Trevon Adams sat on one of couches by the window. He leaned forward with his elbows on his knees, hands clasped, and eyes closed. Brent thought he might be praying, so he didn't try to speak with him. Chennelle's parents and sister were huddled together on a couch on the opposite wall.

"Sergeant Freeman?" said Agent Pan as she entered the waiting area. "I was just told about the attempt on your detective's life. How is she?"

"She's still in surgery. While trying to fight off her attacker, he broke open her wound." Brent looked over his shoulder at Trevon who hadn't changed positions, then lowered his voice. "What really sucks is that her parents and sister came to take her home today and found this."

"Maybe we should go into the hall for a moment," Pan said.

Brent thought this odd at first, but decided if Agent Pan had police business to discuss, they shouldn't do it in front of Chennelle's family. When they were far enough away, Agent Pan spoke to him quietly.

"Sergeant, we think we're finding more links between this

shooting and our case. Dwayne Glover's girlfriend came into the Indianapolis office this morning and told one of our agents Dwayne knew Nina Clemente. She also said she overheard some conversations about some cops who were in on it, but she didn't have any idea of their names."

Brent's head started to ache again. Maybe he should have taken a medical leave after all. He wasn't sure he could take more bad news.

"The FBI is taking over the drive-by," she said.

Shocked, Brent started to say something, but a doctor approaching interrupted him. He saw Agent Pan give the doctor a strange look.

"Are you part of the Kendall family?"

"Actually, I'm her boss and this is FBI Agent Pan. Her family and boyfriend are in the waiting area."

The doctor sighed heavily, which did not bode well. He told them to follow him and they did so.

"Kendall family?" asked the doctor.

All of them rose at once and came forward with anxious faces.

"I'm her mother," said Mrs. Kendall. "How's my baby girl?"

The doctor paused and glanced at the floor. Another bad sign. Brent's heart thumped in his chest, threatening to escape.

"There's no good way to tell you this. We aren't sure how the blood clots formed, whether before or after the attack. Three dislodged and entered her lungs. I'm sorry, she didn't make it."

"What?" said a voice from behind them. Barnes and Samuels were standing there frozen.

"This can't be," said Trevon. "She was supposed to come home today."

"I realize that," said the doctor. "Unfortunately, the episode today changed things. Clots this size do form after surgeries, but often disappear in a few days or weeks. In her struggle to fend off her attacker, they dislodged."

"My poor baby," cried Mrs. Kendall. Her husband put his arms around his wife and daughter. Brent couldn't even remember Chennelle's sister's name.

"When can we see her?" asked Mr. Kendall.

"I'm afraid you can't. The FBI has taken her to Quantico. They need to do an autopsy and collect evidence from the attack."

"Are you serious?" shouted Trevon.

Brent could hear Barnes's heavy breathing and small sobs coming from Samuels. He turned to Agent Pan in disbelief. It was bad enough they'd lost their daughter, now she'd be a thousand miles away.

"I'm sorry, Sergeant Freeman," said Pan. "It's part of the procedure. It's essential we find who is behind this and the FBI has the best equipment to do so."

He turned away from her and went directly to Chennelle's mother. "Mrs. Kendall. Your daughter was a fine detective. The Indianapolis Metropolitan Police Department was very fortunate to have her working with us. I'm so sorry for your loss."

His voice cracked by the time he finished. *Was*…he had to use the word *was* now. He looked over to where Trevon sat on the couch again, this time with his head in his hands.

"Sergeant Freeman…."

"Not now, Agent Pan," he said. "We need to leave these people to their grief. I, for one, am going home for the day. I'll see you tomorrow." Brent motioned for Barnes and Samuels to follow him, leaving Agent Pan in their wake.

Chapter 45

It's a Wonderful Life played away and Maricella could see Nurse Judy's eyes were having a hard time staying open. She kept looking at Haley or Jack to tell her what to do. Haley had told her they would leave tonight, but they had to wait until Daryl left and Nurse Judy slept.

Nurse Judy leaned back in the recliner. Minutes later, she snored softly. Jack rose quietly, putting his finger to his mouth for silence. He placed a blanket over Nurse Judy and dimmed the lights, leaving the television on. Jack gestured for Maricella and Haley to follow him.

"Get your things and meet me in the barn," Jack whispered. "I'm going to the coop to get the backpacks and then to the barn to saddle the horses. Be *very* quiet while you get ready."

The two girls went to their room and collected the pillowcases they'd filled with socks, warm shirts and pants, and several pairs of mittens Haley had found. She told Maricella she thought they were supplies for future children. They also bunched up their blankets with towels under them to make it look like they were in their beds. That was Jack's idea.

After they bundled up, Maricella and Haley met Jack in the barn. They put as many of their clothes into the packs and saddle bags as they could while he went back to the kitchen to grab more food. When he returned, he also had a flashlight for each of them.

"We're going to stick close together, so we'll only use one of these at a time. I grabbed some extra batteries, but we don't want to use them all up the first night. I don't know how long it will take us to find help."

Jack had told them yesterday that, although he'd been in the woods with Daryl, he'd never been anywhere else off the property since he arrived five years ago. He'd seen a lot of kids come and go, but didn't remember anyone as young as Maricella. Now he wanted to save her. She felt lucky to have Jack. It was like having a big brother.

"I took another peek at Judy while I was in there," said Jack. "I wanted to make sure she's still asleep. It's safe to go now."

Haley had made Maricella put on an extra pair of socks, which made her boots really tight. Her snowsuit made it hard to move easily.

"I'm hot," said Maricella.

"You won't be in a minute," said Haley. "Just be glad you don't have to walk in the snow. It will be cold enough up on the horses."

Moments later Haley and Jack had everything ready. Maricella reached for her backpack, but Jack shook his head.

"You'll be sitting in front of me. There won't be room for it," he said. "I can attach it to Haley's saddle. Haley, you carry the flashlight and shine it so we can see where we're going."

Maricella noticed Jack had a rifle slung over his shoulder. "Why do you have a gun?"

"Because there are animals in the woods that are hungry, and I don't plan on being breakfast," he said.

Maricella stopped, frozen in place by fear.

"Come on," said Haley, grabbing Maricella's arm. "We have to get moving."

"Don't jerk her around like that," said Jack. "Come on, Mari. You don't have to be afraid. We'll be okay."

Jack lifted Maricella easily onto the saddle and told her to hold the horn thing while he got on so she wouldn't fall off. Afraid, her thoughts went to Abuela Elena. She pretended they were praying together. God would make sure she got home safely.

Chapter 46

Christmas Eve had dawned brightly, but a gloom hung over Brent as he'd sat silently eating breakfast with Erica and Ben this morning. He couldn't remember a Christmas season that had been quite this depressing. Not even when he was ten and his father disappeared on what he called a private holiday. Later, they'd discovered he'd been on a three-day bender in a rundown motel on the north side of Kokomo.

He hadn't gotten much sleep between his nightmares and hearing Erica crying in the bedroom next door. Not even when he took two Vicodin could he get any rest. He doubted Ben slept much either.

Brent told Erica she could take the day off, but she insisted on working. He'd sent her and Samuels to Forensics to ask if they'd processed anything from Kendall's room before the FBI took it all.

Brent also had a cloud of guilt hanging over his head. Although she didn't say so, he could hear the disappointment in his mother's voice when he called her to ask if they could postpone their Christmas celebration. Because this was her favorite holiday, he told her not to cancel the party. His nieces and nephews shouldn't miss out because of him. He said he'd help her cook a big family dinner on New Years. Luckily, she didn't ask any questions about Natalie.

"Good morning, Sergeant Freeman," said Agent Pan. She had a sad telling look on her face. Another wave of guilt swept over him as he recalled his rudeness of the day before.

"I'm sorry…." he started to say.

"Stop right there," she said. "There is no need to apologize. I know what it's like to lose part of your team."

And she did. Two of the agents she supervised had been murdered outside of the Clemente house just days ago.

Brent relayed all of the information Barnes had given him the night before about Samuels's interview with Carlos Colon. He also handed her the report Samuels had submitted.

Agent Pan flipped through the pages. "It wouldn't surprise me if the girl was taken out of state. Kentucky has a lot of wooded rural areas with miles between houses." She sat down in his side chair and inserted the report in her briefcase then placed it on the floor.

"Here's the sketch the artist drew from Colon's description of Daryl. He looks sort of back woodsy, doesn't he?"

She pursed her lips as she stared at the man in the drawing. "I need to go to the Louisville office. They may be familiar with this man."

"I'd like to go with you," said Brent. Since he wouldn't be going to his hometown for Christmas, he saw no reason not to accompany her and see this thing through.

"Are you sure? I hate for you to cancel your holiday plans."

"I'm sure. I've already told my mother I won't be able to make it until New Years." He handed her the sketch. "You can fax this to their office from here and maybe they'll have something for us by the time we get there."

"Can you be ready to go in a couple of hours?" she asked. "I heard there's a snowstorm developing south of us, so we should get out of here as soon as possible. I can pick you up if you like."

"My suitcases are at my apartment. If I go now, I can pack and meet you at Detective Barnes's house in a couple of hours."

Brent left and went to the apartment he shared with Natalie. He dreaded going back there, but he didn't have enough clothes at Erica's to take on the trip. When he pulled up, he saw no sign of Natalie's car. His speeding heart rate dropped and he took some deep breaths of relief.

When he entered the apartment, he found stacks of boxes. He took a look in one of them and found his books. He hadn't brought much when he moved in. He'd wisely put his furniture and kitchen items in storage and only brought things of comfort, like his books, his baseball card collection, and photos of his family. He went into the bedroom and found his portion of the closet bare along with the drawers that had been his. This was going to complicate packing for his trip to Kentucky.

There were only about ten boxes, so he hauled them down to his vehicle. Luckily, Erica had obtained a rather large SUV for him from the car pool, so everything fit perfectly. He also found his suitcases and the boxes marked *CLOTHING*. When he arrived at Ben and Erica's place, he parked the SUV and only took in the clothing box and a suitcase. He already had his shaving kit there.

He found a couple of suits in the case which weren't too wrinkled and some laundered shirts in the box along with some underwear and socks. He'd just shut his suitcase when the doorbell rang.

"I see you couldn't wait to get your things," shouted Natalie as she pushed her way in. "How dare you come to the apartment without my permission."

"I needed to get some clothes, I'm…."

"You took more than that! Oh, and what's the suitcase for? You going to Kokomo or did you make other plans?"

Brent looked away from her, his heart beating furiously. Trying unsuccessfully to hold his temper, he turned on her. "You're the one who packed up everything. You're the one who told me to find somewhere else to sleep two days ago. Now you have the nerve to come in here screaming at me because I took my own things."

"You should have arranged to come pick them up."

"I had no idea I had boxes to *pick up*. I thought you just needed to cool off, but it's obvious now you're done with me. But you know what? I'm glad. I'm sick and tired of your jealous snipes at my female colleagues and friends. You'd think with all you've accomplished, you'd have more confidence. I wanted this relationship to work, but I can't be with someone who refuses to trust me."

Again, the doorbell rang; he knew things were about to get worse. This had to be Agent Pan coming to pick him up.

"I'm going to the FBI office in Louisville this afternoon to try to find a little girl before she's butchered," he said, pushing himself to speak calmly. "We have a lead and I'm going to follow it."

The doorbell rang again. He reached in his pocket and pulled out his key ring. He removed the apartment key and handed it to her. "My ride is here so you'll need to leave."

Natalie grabbed the key, scraping his fingers. She flung open the door to a shocked Agent Pan. "Louisville?" said Natalie. "Whatever." Then she flew past Agent Pan, bumping her roughly as she went by. Tires screeched as Natalie sped off.

"Long story," he said retrieving his suitcase.

Pan smiled at him. "We've got a two to three hour trip ahead of us, so I'm all ears if you want to talk about it."

"Thanks," he said. Brent thought he'd be more upset than this, but strangely he only felt relieved.

Chapter 47

"I'm hungry," said Maricella. Her tummy growled and her legs ached from straddling the saddle for so long. Even with the extra socks and mittens, her fingers and toes were really cold.

"There's a tree stand up ahead," said Jack. "We can go up there and get some rest and eat."

"It's about time," said Haley. "But if we're in a tree, where are the horses going to stay?"

Maricella thought that was a good question. "Won't the bad animals hurt them?" she asked.

"I don't think so, Mari, but better them than us," he said. "I'll keep an eye out and shoot them if they try to attack our rides."

"There it is," he said. "Good, I thought I remembered this one having a ladder. Mari, let's get down. I'll put this smaller pack on your back and you climb up first. Then you, Haley. It will probably be covered in some snow, so we'll need to try to knock it off."

The girls did as they were told with Jack bringing up the rear. It was really hard to climb with cold fingers and toes, but Maricella did it. A thin layer of snow did cover about half of the platform. She thought the sun had melted some of it, since it could peek through the leafless trees now.

Jack finally arrived. "This is good. I'll spread the sleeping bag over here where the snow's melted. I'll push the rest off and it should dry soon. We can see for miles that way, where we came from. If anyone's coming we can get down and get started again."

"If you can see them, won't they be too close for us to get away?" asked Haley.

"Haley, you worry too much and ask too many questions," he said. Jack spread out a really big sleeping bag. "This is a double bag, but as small as the two of you are, we should all fit in it. Sharing body heat will keep us alive. You two go ahead and get in, but take off your boots. We don't want it getting wet inside."

Maricella took off her boots and quickly got into the bag. Once Haley joined her, it didn't take long for her to warm up. She watched as Jack put their boots into plastic bags and then started pulling out food.

"We're going to need to eat some protein to sustain our energy," he said. He handed them some strange looking strips that looked like something one of Maricella's friends used to give her dog. "Haven't you ever had beef jerky before, Mari?" he asked.

She shook her head and sniffed it. Then she took a tiny bite. It tasted kind of salty, and she had to chew it for a long time, but she liked it. She'd decided if Jack ate it, so would she.

After a meal of beef jerky, dried fruits, and nuts with some water to wash it down, Maricella started to feel sleepy.

"Okay, you girls get some sleep and I'll keep watch." He picked up the bags with the boots in them. "Slip these down in the bag so they get warm. Also, pull off your extra socks, your coats and the snowsuit's leggings while you're in there, but keep them in there with you so they don't get cold. This sleeping bag reflects your body heat. You'll get too warm if you have all that on."

Jack was right. As soon as Maricella burrowed down in the sleeping bag, she had to take off her socks and coat. This was amazing. She worried about Jack, though. He had put his legs into the sleeping bag, too, but had to keep his head out to watch. She put her arm across his knee and he patted her on the head. Soon she slept and dreamt of home.

When Jack shook them awake, Maricella felt confused at first. She had thought Mamá was waking her to come open presents. Instead, she woke to snowflakes falling and Jack slipping his boots back on."

"We've got to get moving," he said. "I'm sure Judy is awake by now and she'll be calling Daryl. We have to get a better head start on him."

Jack looked really worried. Maricella thought he wanted to hurry because of the snow as well as because of Daryl. He'd said it would be harder for them if the weather got worse. Once they were packed and out of the tree, Jack turned to them.

"You girls go over there and use the bathroom real quick while I get the horses ready. By the time they catch up to here, the snow should have covered up our new tracks. Hopefully, Chaser won't be able to find our trail either."

Chaser. Maricella hadn't thought of that. She's seen dogs on TV who could find people, but some of them jumped and bit the bad people. She wondered if Chaser would do that to her.

Going to the bathroom was the worst. It was hard not to get her clothes wet, and her bottom got so cold. She hurried as fast as she could with Haley's help and then they met back up with Jack. Haley tightened Maricella's scarf around her face and then Jack put her back in the saddle.

The snow increased. At least there wasn't a strong wind blowing. New snow would fill in the hoof prints, but it would also make it more difficult for the horses to walk as it got deeper. Since she'd prayed for God's help, maybe this would be his way of making it hard for anybody to follow them. She had to trust Him to take care of her.

Chapter 48

Lin walked into the rear of the house to find it astonishingly quiet. She pulled off her boots in the mudroom and slipped on her shoes. Something wasn't right. She could feel it.

Entering the kitchen, she saw no signs of breakfast dishes. As a matter of fact, the pots and pans in the drainer looked more like something in which dinner would have been prepared.

"Jack," she called. No response. She went back to the mudroom. The boots, coats, and even Maricella's snowsuit were missing. Looking out the door, she saw no footprints leading to the barn or chicken coop, but it had been snowing for about an hour now.

"Judy! Jack! Haley!" Panic set in. Judy's car was in the drive covered with snow. Where were they all? Then she heard a groan coming from the living room. Rushing in, she found Judy holding her head and moaning.

"Judy. Where are the children?"

"What?"

Judy didn't seem very coherent. Lin grabbed her and pulled her into a sitting position.

"What the…Lin, what are you doing here? Are the children having breakfast?

"No. I want to know where they are."

"Maybe they're still in bed," said Judy, her squint indicating a headache.

Lin shook her violently. "Have you been drinking? Did you pass out last night?"

Judy pushed Lin's hands away and stood up, putting some distance between them, but stumbled slightly. She seemed confused.

"I asked you a question," said Lin. "Did you decide to have some holiday cheer and get drunk last night?"

"Are you serious? I rarely drink and I sure wouldn't do it when I'm working. Although…," Judy's words trailed off.

Lin's anger fumed, ready to explode. She left the room before she did something she might regret and headed for the bedrooms. Her most important asset at the moment was Maricella. Both beds appeared to be occupied, but when Lin pulled back the blankets all she found were towels and toys bunched up underneath. She ripped the blankets off Haley's bed to find the same things.

Howling in anger, she ran to Jack's room. Again, no one occupied the bed. She returned to the hallway ready to rip her own hair out and saw Judy at the top of the stairs. Hot with fury, she approached Judy who cringed against the wall. Lin brought her arm up and pinned Judy against the wall by the throat.

"The children are gone. If you weren't drinking, how do you explain the way you are acting this morning?"

She could feel Judy shaking as she tried to pull Lin's arm away from her throat. Lin brought her face so close to Judy's that their noses almost touched.

"Stop struggling." Lin loosened the pressure slightly. "I could snap your neck with one quick gesture, but it won't help me find the children, will it?" Then she released Judy, backing away from her.

Judy shook her head, tears began to stream down her cheeks. Her voice became rough and raspy. "I don't know what happened. The children and I were watching a movie on television when Jack offered to make me some tea. He said it would help me relax."

"What kind of tea?"

"He said it was herbal. Something they grow out here. I thought it was chamomile tea, but it would never knock me out like this did."

"What time was it?"

Judy rubbed her neck along the red streak Lin had left. "Near the end of the movie, so probably close to nine-thirty."

"I suppose Daryl decided to go Lexington."

Judy nodded. "Yes. He said he'd return tomorrow morning. I'm sorry. I thought the children would be excited about Christmas. I saw no indications that they were unhappy or might be getting ready to do something like this."

"Call Daryl and tell him I'm here and he's to return immediately," demanded Lin.

"I suspect they'd have taken a path through the woods. Daryl is a hunter. He should be able to find them rather quickly." Judy looked almost gleeful at the prospect.

"You'd better hope he finds them alive and healthy. I would give you a quick death, but if my father finds out about this…let's just say you wouldn't be so lucky."

Chapter 49

"Samuels, there's one thing you need to know about Dr. Brian Palmer—he's a super scientific nerd who will talk incessantly if you let him. He's very good at his job and he knows it."

Anne knew Dr. Palmer as IMPD's expert DNA analyst, but had no reason to interact with him directly until now. She and Barnes were hoping he, or someone in Forensics, had been able to start testing before the FBI swooped in on the Kendall murder case.

They found him sitting at his computer intently peering at the screen. His wavy blond hair set a stark contrast for his thick-rimmed black glasses. He did look like the stereotypical nerd. It didn't appear he'd heard them come in, that is until Barnes let the door slam shut. Anne and Dr. Palmer both flinched at the sound. Anne had discovered that Barnes had a little bit of a mean streak.

"Hey, Brian. Have you met Detective Anne Samuels yet?"

Dr. Palmer removed his glasses, smiled, and reached for Anne's hand. She couldn't help but see he had very nice crystal blue eyes. Without the glasses, he looked more like a surfer than a nerd.

"Nice to meet you," he said. "What can I do for you, detectives?"

It felt like a, *you use my proper title and I'll use yours,* statement. With his education and expertise, Anne felt he deserved it despite Barnes's propensity to mock him.

"Samuels and I are working the shootings of Glover, Flores, and Kendall, as well as the hospital attack on the latter. Did you or anyone in the lab have a chance to collect or process any evidence from the hospital before the FBI took over?"

"For some reason, they were on scene pretty quickly. None of our guys even got to examine the....you know, after the surgery. The coroner wasn't even allowed in."

"I don't suppose they found any DNA on anything from the original murder case?"

"No. The bullets that hit the victims and the buildings were too damaged to get any good fingerprints from them. If we had the weapon, we might have been able to collect DNA from it. Sorry. I know Mark Chatham has been working long hours on these cases."

"Do you know if he's in this morning?" asked Barnes.

"I'm not sure, but you can check his office. I rarely see anyone unless they bring evidence for me to test."

"Thanks, Brian," said Barnes. "Let's go, Samuels."

They walked down the hall to Mark Chatham's office. Anne had a little crush on him, but had decided not to pursue it, even though he worked in a completely different area than she did. After watching Sergeant Freeman's relationship with Prosecutor Ralston crumble, she knew she'd made the right decision.

"Hey, Mark," said Barnes.

He frowned at her. "Before you ask, no, I have absolutely nothing substantial on your homicides except for ballistics. The bullets were 9 mils shot from a TEC-DC9."

"That gun's banned from being sold," said Barnes.

"Yeah, it is," he said. He sat back in his chair looking angry. "Shut the door."

Anne turned and closed his door. She and Barnes took the seats in front of his desk. Then Chatham leaned forward and spoke in a very low voice.

"We've got a dirty cop. Ballistics shows the gun used should have been in our inventory. It's missing."

"I was afraid of that," said Barnes. "Any idea who's been in the area lately?"

"I have a list." He reached in his drawer and pulled out a file. "Here you go. I don't envy you this task, but you'll want to have a chat with Major Stevenson about this one."

Barnes took the folder and sighed. "My gut told me there had to be someone on the inside involved. Who else would have known about Flores and Kendall's plans to meet up with Glover?"

"Good question," said Anne. She knew Detective Barnes's first suspect—Lewis Paxton from Gangs. He had been much too nosey when they asked Jackson for information on Glover. It wasn't his case or his snitch. Maybe Barnes's instincts were correct.

"Let's go see how Major Stevenson wants us to handle this one, Samuels," said Barnes. "When one of your own goes bad, things get very complicated."

Chapter 50

Lin unlocked her desk drawer and pulled out a bottle of vodka and a glass. She needed a drink to calm her nerves. Pouring the sparkling, colorless liquid, her mind flashed to her conversation with her father. If flames could shoot through a phone, she'd be cooked. Lin had assured him she had everything under control. If she weren't his daughter, she'd be getting a visit from Zeng and would end up like Nina.

To her relief, her father agreed to give Judy one more chance as well after she told him about the spiked tea. It had been difficult to find a nurse who would agree to work for them. This one's mother was in an assisted living facility and cost her at least eight thousand a month. Judy couldn't pass up such a hefty paycheck, despite the risks.

Lin heard a door slam and a male voice yelling. "What the hell happened, Judy?"

Swigging down the last of her drink, Lin rose and walked out to the kitchen to find Daryl glaring at Judy. She slammed the glass down on the counter, getting their attention.

"What happened, Mr. Townsend, is the boy in *your* charge has run off and taken the merchandise with him. My father is not pleased." Lin paced, pursing her lips and clinching her fists. "In order for you to keep his favor, you must find them and bring them back. What you do with your boy is up to you. Maricella needs to be treated like a china doll, but the other girl is expendable should she give you any trouble."

"You do know how hard it is to get a blonde haired, blue eyed, white girl, don't you?" he asked.

"I'm sure it's quite difficult. However, the price we will get for Maricella's organs will far exceed the profit for Haley. Besides, you are paid very well for your services and should not complain about how hard it is to do your job."

Lin could see Daryl's Adam's apple bob nervously. She'd made her point. If he didn't want to suffer Nina's fate, he'd do as she instructed.

Daryl left the room and Lin went to the window. Snow continued to fall as night drew near. The children had been gone for at least sixteen hours now. How much rest had they gotten? Had Daryl trained the boy in survival? Despite the fact they were on horseback, the snow had surely slowed them down.

Daryl returned with a rifle in his hands.

"Is that necessary?" asked Judy.

"One of my rifles and some bullets are missing, so yeah, it's necessary. I ain't lettin' that little weasel shoot me. I'll saddle up Clyde first thing tomorrow...."

"You'll go now." Lin felt the heat rising in her face. They'd been gone too long already. "You've said yourself their chances for survival are slim in this weather. I want Maricella back now. I put Dr. Sun off until tomorrow. You'd both better hope his clients didn't get the merchandise from someone else."

Daryl glanced down at the floor, shaking his head. "Let me go get my night vision goggles and pack up. It'll probably be dark before I can set out."

"Then don't just stand there, do it!" Lin's temper grew shorter by the minute as she watched him go out the door.

"I wonder why the children didn't take all of the horses," commented Judy.

"According to Daryl, *Clyde* hates Jack. He was only eight when he came to us, but we thought he'd do well taking care of the animals until we could get the money from the buyer. Unfortunately, the first time Jack went out to feed that wretched beast, it bit a chunk out of his arm. You can't sell damaged merchandise, so we gave him to Daryl as a farm hand."

Lin strolled over to the counter and grabbed her glass. "I'll be in my office. Do not disturb me until he returns with Maricella."

Chapter 51

"When we meet with Agent Smythe, let me do the talking," said Agent Pan. "He's a bit territorial. You being from Indianapolis instead of local...well...he might respond to me better."

Brent sighed. "We all want the same results."

"I know, but not everyone wants to share and play nice."

Brent and Agent Pan entered the Federal Building and made their way through the checkpoints before ascending to Agent Smythe's office on the third floor. As they rode up in the elevator, he thought of his mother and sisters. He'd never missed a Christmas Eve with them before.

The elevator doors slid open and Brent followed Agent Pan through a desk-ridden area where only a few were occupied. Pan had to convince Agent Smythe to see them before leaving. Brent thought she did a fine job of putting the *what if it was your daughter who was missing at Christmas* guilt trip on him.

A tall thin man with coffee brown hair graying at the temples greeted them. "Agent Pan. May I assume you are Sergeant Freeman?" he asked.

Brent nodded and shook Smythe's hand, remembering Agent Pan's instructions not to speak. She probably didn't mean he had to go this far, but why take chances?

"Agent Smythe, did you get a chance to check out the sketch I faxed to you before we left Indianapolis?" she asked.

"As a matter of fact, I did. Come into my office. I have the person of interest on my computer screen."

They entered his office and he invited them to come around his desk, giving Agent Pan his chair. On screen, the photo showed a skinny, unshaven man with hair down to his shoulders. Agent Smythe had a scanned copy of the sketch on screen as well. With the exception of the hair length, they could be the same person. Even to the mole near his right eye.

"His name is Daryl Townsend. He lives on a large piece of property south of here near Taylorsville. It butts up against Lake State Park. His property has at least an acre of woods between the house and the border of the park. There are also five acres of woods on either side of the property, which makes surveillance very difficult."

"You still have people watching the property at the road, right?" asked Pan.

"Yes. This is what makes us suspicious of his involvement with the trafficking ring. As a matter of fact, Lin Huang herself has been seen coming and going this past week."

"Who is Lin Huang?" asked Brent.

"Han Wu's only child," answered Smythe.

"Interesting." Agent Pan leaned back in her chair, staring intently at the screen. "It says here one of his known associates was Nina Clemente."

"Right. I heard someone murdered her in Indianapolis the day after she left Townsend's property."

"Clemente's murder happened days after two young girls were kidnapped and the mother of the youngest child was murdered." Pan rose from her chair and went to the window.

"There's more," said Smythe. "Surveillance ran a license plate of a new arrival. The vehicle's owned by Judy Klaussen. She arrived the day after Clemente left. She's a nurse who's been making some pretty hefty bank deposits lately. Of course, the money's going out as soon as it goes in. Checks are going to an Alzheimer's nursing facility here in Louisville."

"Mom or Dad must be a patient," said Agent Pan.

"Mom," said Smythe. "Right now we believe Klaussen's there alone with the children. Our agents reported that Townsend left yesterday and hasn't returned. Huang left two days ago."

"These girls are only twelve and five," said Pan. "I think you can guess what they want from a five-year-old." She turned and met Smythe's eyes. He frowned and dropped his gaze.

"That's why I'm here instead of at home with my family," said Agent Smythe. "Since you have an eye witness who described this Daryl, we have probable cause to search his property. I've already asked for a warrant, not an easy task on Christmas Eve. I've got a team ready to take you down there as soon as we have the warrant. Problem now is, it's getting dark."

"You know what they say about cover of darkness," said Pan. "If the Klaussen woman is truly alone with them, she won't be able to make a break for it before we sneak up on her. The sooner we get out there the better."

"It's snowing too hard to send you in a helicopter, so you'll have to go by car. Hope you brought warm boots, Sergeant. You're going to need them."

Chapter 52

"Barnes! Samuels! In my office," barked Major Stevenson. Anne jumped out of her chair and quickly followed Barnes.

"Close the door," he said. He pointed to the chairs in front of his desk and sat in the one behind it. "Detective Barnes, it appears you may be correct about Detective Paxton. He visited the evidence room the day before the shooting."

"Have you talked with his commander?" asked Barnes.

"I didn't tell him why I wanted to talk to Paxton, but he told me Paxton went home sick," said the major. "I suspect he knows we've discovered his secret. The man's been a cop for fifteen years. How could he possibly think we'd never discover he'd taken a gun from the evidence locker, which we'll assume he used in this shooting?"

"Desperate people don't think," said Anne. She noticed Detective Barnes gave her a reassuring nod.

"Exactly," said Stevenson. "It appears he also attacked Kendall at the hospital in desperation. The FBI lab confirmed the skin under her fingernails matched Paxton's DNA. He may have thought she saw him during the shooting."

"So what now?" asked Barnes.

"We have a couple of patrol officers watching his house. They've seen him go past the window a couple of times, but our main concern is his family." Major Stevenson got out of his chair and gazed out the window. "I want the two of you to make the arrest. Even if we don't have sufficient evidence to make the murder charges for Glover and Flores, Kendall provided us with plenty of evidence in her case when she scratched him." He turned to face them. "The one thing we don't want is a hostage situation, but we'll be sending in SWAT just in case."

"Then may I assume we will be doing this immediately?" asked Barnes.

"Yes. You two need to wear your vests and make sure your weapons are at the ready. You'll have earpieces for communication. Be careful. If he was desperate enough to participate in a drive by and kill two cops, he'll be even more desperate now. He won't hesitate to take out two more."

"Let's go, Samuels. We need to gear up."

* * * * *

The SWAT vehicles were parked a block away. Everyone prepared for the worst case scenario. Their commander went over a map of the area with his team, then summoned Anne and Detective Barnes over.

"It's my understanding you two have been assigned to knock on the door and make the arrest. Here's the plan." He showed them the map of the area. "You will drive up and park on the street. It will give you some cover if he sees you and decides to shoot before you get up to the house. We'll have vehicles coming from both directions. Under no circumstances should you enter the residence. He's got a wife and twin nine-year-old daughters in there. If his wife answers the door, you tell her to ask her husband to come outside, got it?"

"And if he has one of them with a gun to her head?" asked Anne.

"You draw your weapons and ask him to put his down. If he doesn't do it, you run for cover and we'll take over. We've got a negotiator with us who will call him and try to talk him down."

"You good, Samuels?" asked Barnes.

Anne was terrified, but she nodded. Detective Barnes had such a calm demeanor on the outside, but could she be trembling on the inside?

Anne and Erica rode up to the house in silence. Already dark out, Anne saw most of the house lights were on. Maybe Paxton wasn't feeling well, or maybe he faked being sick to be home with his family early. She hoped they had the element of surprise on their side.

They got out of the car and approached the house. Barnes whispered, "Unsnap your holster and be sharp. No telling what Paxton is thinking right now."

Barnes rang the doorbell and motioned for Anne to move so she stood slightly left of the door. She watched for the porch light to go on, but it didn't. Quick light footsteps approached. When the door opened, a short blond woman sporting a red sweater, jeans, and white Rudolph apron stared at them.

The woman appeared to be confused. She looked them up and down when Detective Barnes flashed her badge. "How may I help you?"

"We need to speak with Detective Paxton," said Barnes. "It's rather urgent. Can you ask him to come outside, please?"

"Hello, Detectives." The deep male voice had come from behind. "Would you be so kind as to go inside?"

Chapter 53

The sun had set and the snow had let up. Jack pointed out a little hunting shack straight ahead. He'd told Maricella they were very lucky to find it. The sun had been gone a long time and it got hard to see in the dark, even with a flashlight. It looked run down, but it would be a good place to stop for the night. Maricella was cold and hungry.

Inside, they found a small wooden table and chairs. They were dirty, but would be okay for their needs. A small woodpile sat next to a big black thing Jack called a potbelly stove. She'd never heard of one of those before. Jack didn't really want to start it up, because of the smoke. However, the place didn't seem much warmer than outside, just drier.

"Girls, go ahead and unpack just what you need. We'll put our wet clothes over here by the stove so they can dry. Once the fire's going I'll fix us some of this soup. That should warm you up."

"Let me help you, Mari," said Haley.

Maricella glared at her, starting to feel really cranky. "I'm not a baby. I can get my own stuff."

"Suit yourself," said Haley. "Roll out your sleeping bag. We'll need to get some sleep soon." She turned to Jack. "How long do you think we have before Daryl gets home and starts looking for us?"

"Even if Judy called Daryl this morning, the new snow should slow him down. He can't get his snowmobile through those trees, but he can ride that hateful horse of his." Jack pulled out a pan and two cans of soup, a can of pears, and a bottle of water from his pack. "Clyde's big enough to trudge through the snow real easy. I just hope Daryl waits until daylight to come after us."

"But the snow covered most of our tracks," said Haley.

"It won't matter if he brings Chaser."

"Is Chaser a really good hunter?" asked Maricella.

"Chaser is a great hunter. He'll be able to sniff us out no matter how much snow there is. Here, eat so we can get some sleep."

Jack had brought tin cups for the soup; it warmed Maricella from head to toe. They passed around the can of pears, which she thought tasted sweet and cold. She'd never had to share food out of a can before. She wondered if people lived like this in the olden days.

"Get in your sleeping bag," ordered Jack. "We need to go to sleep for a few hours. Whoever wakes up first needs to wake the others, okay?"

"Sure," said Haley.

Once Jack turned off the flashlight, the soft glow coming from the stove became the only light in the room. Between the heat from it and the sleeping bag, Maricella became quite warm and comfortable. Her eyes began to flutter, and she could feel her body relaxing when suddenly a loud bark made her sit up. Heart pounding in her chest, she could barely see Jack as he jumped to his feet and retrieved the rifle. He checked it for bullets.

Maricella shook from fear. "Is that Chaser?"

"Shhh. I don't know, but it sounds like him. You two go hide in the corner and...."

The door burst open and a bright light blinded her. Jack turned, gun raised, but Daryl was faster. The blast from his weapon hurt Maricella's ears. She covered her head while Haley clung to her and screamed. When she dared to open her eyes, she heard Jack moaning and saw him clinging to his leg.

"Thought you's a big shot, did ya boy?" Daryl picked up the rifle Jack had brought, a bright light shining from his head. "Ya mighta had a chance if ya weren't so stupid. How many times I tell ya to flip the safety switch?"

"You didn't have to shoot him!" screamed Haley.

"Shut up, girl, before I give you the same thing."

Maricella began to cry. This was horrible. Worse than anything she'd imagined. How did Daryl find them so quickly? Jack rolled in pain. This had to be her fault. He'd be safe at home now if he hadn't tried to save her.

"You two get up and come here," said Daryl. "I should be able to haul you both back since I got two more horses now."

"What about Jack?" said Haley. "He's hurt. You have to take him, too."

"Never mind about Jack. He disobeyed me so he can just lay here and bleed to death."

"You can't do that! You have to take him back with us."

Maricella thought Haley very brave for talking back to Daryl, but he looked extremely angry. She knew the look. It was the one she saw on her Papá's face almost all the time.

Jack gritted his teeth and held his hand over his shin where it continued to bleed. "Haley, just do what he says. Leave me."

"Well, well, maybe you're not so dumb after all. What the...."

While Jack had Daryl's attention, Haley ran at him full force with a piece of firewood. Unfortunately, she only knocked him off balance. Daryl brought up the handle of his rifle and hit her in the face. She fell to the floor, her eyes closed as if she was asleep.

"Haley," screamed Maricella. She ran to her and shook her. "Wake up, please, please."

Daryl grabbed Maricella by the arm and dragged her away. He pulled some rope he had hanging from his shoulder and tied Haley's arms and legs. Then he did the same to Jack.

Maricella watched, unable to move. She feared what would happen to her if she did. The tears made her face ice cold. Her papá made her mamá go to sleep like that once, but she got better. Of course, Abuela Elena had taken her mamá to the hospital. There wasn't anyone around to take care of Haley and Jack.

"Okay, girl. Looks like it's just you and me and the horses. I'll leave Chaser here to keep an eye on them." He yanked Maricella up from the floor and took her outside.

Clyde snorted, steam coming out of his nose. He was even taller than the horse she'd ridden with Jack. She wasn't sure how she'd get up there, but Daryl lifted her up easily then pulled himself up on the saddle behind her. Then he rode up to each of the other two horses and gave each a smack on their hind quarters. They ran off, Daryl and Maricella following them.

"Where are they going?" asked Maricella.

"These is smart horses, girl. They know their way home where the food is. I bet that stupid kid didn't even think to bring them food."

She didn't remember Jack bringing anything for them.

"You know horse stealin' is against the law, don't you?"

Maricella shook her head, suddenly afraid she might have to go to jail just like Papá did. "Why did you hurt Jack and Haley?" she asked.

"You know why," he said. "They caused a lot of trouble. Bad children get punished."

"Where are we going?"

"Back to my house. Lin's waitin' for ya."

Chapter 54

"Lew, what's going on?" asked Mrs. Paxton. "Who are they and…." She paused, looking horror struck. "Lew, why do you have a gun?"

"Becky, I want you to take the girls and go on to your mother's like we planned."

"You're not going with us?" Mrs. Paxton's voice sounded shaky and tears of fear fell from her dark brown eyes.

"Ma'am, you should listen to your husband," said Barnes, her voice calm and steady. "Take your girls and get out of here."

"But I don't want to leave here without my husband."

Anne's heart pounded at the idea of what Detective Paxton would do if pushed too far by his wife's insistence. At this point, he at least had the decency to try to get her out, but she was being way too stubborn for her own good.

"Mrs. Paxton, I'm Detective Anne Samuels and this is Detective Erica Barnes. We have to speak with your husband before he can go anywhere, so for your sake and for your daughters', please leave now."

Becky looked at her husband one more time and then went to the stairway. "Girls, it's time to go to Grandma's."

Two young girls came bounding down the stairs, meeting their mother at the bottom. First telling them to go and get in the car, she then said Daddy had to work a little more and he'd come to Grandma's later.

After hearing the garage door open and close and a vehicle leave the area, Paxton finally spoke. "Okay ladies, I want to start with you, Detective Barnes. Take your weapon out of your holster by the butt with your thumb and index finger and lay it on the coffee table then back up two feet with your fingers locked behind your head. Once she's done, you do the same Detective Samuels. If one of you shoots me, I shoot your partner."

They did as they were told and then he directed them into the dining room. He told them to take seats at the table. "I apologize for not offering you refreshments, but as you can see, you caught me as I was about to take a trip with my family."

"Why'd you go after Kendall?" asked Barnes.

"Who says I did?"

Barnes leaned forward, scowling fiercely. "Your DNA."

He sat there quietly for a few minutes, waving his gun around. Anne hoped the thing wouldn't go off while he did this.

"Why did you go after Glover in the first place?" asked Barnes. "Did he know you're dirty? What about Javier Arroyo? Kendall and Flores went to ask Glover about Arroyo. Did you kill him, too?"

"You think you've got it all worked out, don't you, Barnes? Miss squeaky clean with her high and mighty attitude. Never been tempted to go off the path of righteousness? It must be nice to be so perfect."

Barnes's eyes flared. "I'm not perfect, Paxton. Nobody is. But I do try very hard to always do what's right. I'm supposed to serve and protect the people of Indianapolis. I swore to do it, just as you did. I take *my* oath seriously."

Paxton's laugh made Anne's skin crawl. He'd obviously lost

his mind. Didn't he understand what he now faced?

"Well, I guess this means I'm done, doesn't it?" he asked with a huge grin on his face. He seemed to be enjoying all of this.

"Yeah," said Barnes. "I'm afraid you are. You do realize we didn't come here alone."

"I do."

"Then you may as well give us the whole story," said Anne. If she was going to die, she at least wanted to know the reasons behind it all.

"Sure, why not. It won't matter in a few minutes anyway." He leaned back in his chair, his hand with the gun resting on the table. "It started when the twins came along. Becky had a rough pregnancy and the girls came prematurely. You can imagine how fast the bills stacked up when you have two babies in the natal intensive care unit for three months. The best insurance in the world doesn't pay it all."

Anne glanced at Detective Barnes. Since they were wired, she hoped others were listening and coming up with a strategy to get them out of there.

"I grabbed Carlos Colon on a domestic. He starts telling me and Franco Pinelli how he can get us some extra cash if we'll let him go."

"Pinelli died in an alley six years ago," said Barnes. "Blunt force trauma case that went cold."

"Colon did it," said Paxton. "Pinelli followed me that night because I'd already told him about my debts. He thought I'd take Colon up on his offer. He was right, of course. He confronted me in the alley and Colon bashed him in the back of the head with a baseball bat."

"I guess we can add murder to Colon's other charges," said Anne. "Do you know what happened to Colon's brother-in-law?"

"Carlos pressured him to join Los Hombres. I guess one night Arroyo overheard a conversation between Carlos and Glover. They were talking about trafficking kids and the stupid boy told them he would go to the police. Colon asked me to meet with Arroyo and shut him up. I only planned to put the fear of God into him, but he grabbed my gun and it went off. Not my gun, actually, another gun I'd pulled from the evidence locker. It disappeared in the White River."

Sweat trickled down Paxton's cheek. Then his eyes glazed over. He became calm, much too calm for the situation he found himself in at the moment.

"Colon and Glover were from different gangs. How did they wind up working together?" asked Barnes.

"Neither of their gangs wanted in on the human trafficking if they had to work with the Chinese. The two of them decided to do it independently. The Chinese paid big money, especially for really young ones. The gangs didn't want anything to do with grabbing little kids."

"That's noble of them. But you and your boys thought it was okay, right? Do you have any idea what they're doing with those *young ones*?" asked Barnes. The crease between her eyes showed her anger. "They butcher them and sell their organs to the highest bidder for transplants."

Paxton's face contorted in pain. He'd obviously never bothered to learn the details of the operation for which he worked.

"That's right, Paxton. They take little girls and boys younger than your two, carve them up, and send them in pieces to the vital organs black market," said Barnes. "Of course, they sell the little girls and boys the age of your daughters to perverts who turn them into slaves or worse."

"Stop it!" He stood so quickly he knocked over his chair. His calm demeanor had vanished.

"What did you think they were doing with them?" asked Anne.

"Putting them up for adoption?" She couldn't believe this guy.

"No…I didn't know…I didn't want to know. I did it for my family."

"So what happens to your family now?" asked Anne.

Paxton paced back and forth several times. He stopped abruptly and slowly turned to address them. "They'll be better off without me." Then he placed the gun under his chin and fired before Anne could move to stop him.

Chapter 55

Brent, Pan, and six of the Louisville office agents made their way through the edge of the woods on the west side of Townsend's property. As dawn broke, Brent hoped they still had the element of surprise on their side. It had taken longer to find a judge to sign the warrant than they had anticipated, and the weather had made travel difficult.

The troop stopped when they had nearly reached the open area where the house, barn, and other buildings stood. They needed to spread out more so they could attack from all sides. Winter left them little cover, even in the thickness of the trees. The beauty of the newly fallen snow only provided a background of white that would betray them. The eerie quiet of the area made Brent think the occupants of the house still slept.

Agent Pan started giving instructions. "You three, you're Team One. Watch for any activity coming into the area down the driveway. Everybody make sure your communicator earpieces are secure. Let's test them."

Brent listened as she turned away and tested all of the coils. These were so much better than walkie-talkies. Each consisted of a simple earpiece and a long coil that lead to the small round mouthpiece clipped to their collars. All of it hands free.

Agent Pan continued with her instructions. "If you see anyone, give us your number and then the number of adults and children you see and brief location."

Pan motioned for everyone else to follow her. She left the next trio about the halfway point. She and Brent took a position close to the barn on the east side of the property where they could see the barn and the back of the house. Pan tapped his arm and pointed at two saddled horses standing next to the barn.

Once everyone took their position, they settled in and waited for further instruction. Luckily, a large snowdrift gave Brent and Agent Pan cover. It wasn't long before Brent heard the snap of a branch and a man's gruff voice.

"Well, little girl, let's put old Clyde to bed, and then we'll go inside and get warm. Maybe old Nurse Judy will even make you a cup of hot chocolate."

Brent saw a man on horseback moving slowly across the snow not five feet away from them. He held a child firmly in front of him on the saddle. Brent assumed this must be Daryl Townsend. He glanced at Agent Pan, who shrugged at him. The hood of the man's parka and the bundling of a scarf around it made it hard to see his face. Brent couldn't understand what they had been doing in the woods at this time of day. Nor could he fathom why two other horses were saddled and waiting outside the barn.

"We have to go get Jack and Haley," said the little girl. "They're hurt. Nurse Judy needs to help them."

Brent couldn't see her face because of the hood of her coat, but by her size he guessed this was Maricella Colon. He thought for a moment about the fact there may be two more people hurt in the woods. Then it came to him. They must have tried to run away and Daryl caught up with them. But why only bring Maricella back? Did the others struggle and get injured in the process?

"Never you mind about those brats," said Townsend as he gripped the back of the girls coat and shook her. "They was stupid. I left Chaser to keep an eye on 'em. I'll go check on 'em later. You just worry about how mad Lin's going to be when you go inside."

Brent watched as Townsend rode up to the barn and then

dismounted. He slid one side of the barn door open and the other two horses entered. Then he pulled the girl off the horse. Brent couldn't hear what they were saying now, but he saw Townsend grab Maricella's arm and drag her along with one hand and lead the horse he called Clyde into the barn with the other.

Agent Pan leaned her head toward her mouthpiece. "Team Two, we have one male adult and one small female child entering the barn in the back of the property. From the conversation we overheard, there are at least two adult females in the house," said Pan. "I want you to split. One of you cover the back of the barn, the other two take the east and west sides of it. Sergeant Freeman and I will take the front."

"This is Team Two. We copy."

"Team One, surround the house. One of you goes into the front door, one takes the back door. One of you will stay outside near the garage to make sure no one tries to get to a vehicle."

Team One confirmed. Pan gave the order to go and they reached the barn in time to see Daryl about to exit. Daryl spotted them and grabbed Maricella, lifting her easily. He quickly backed into the barn and closed the door.

Brent heard the lock slide shut. This had now turned into a hostage situation.

Chapter 56

"This is Team One. We have both women in custody. There are no others in the house. How shall we proceed?"

Brent glanced at Pan. How would they be proceeding? Daryl Townsend returned with only one child and he'd overhead Maricella say the other children were hurt.

Pan spoke into her mouthpiece. "You and your partner stay in the house with the suspects. Call it in and request at least two ambulances. According to the child with the third suspect in the barn, there are two other children still in the woods who are injured."

Pan closed her eyes and lowered her head for a moment. "I want the agent watching the garage to join us at the front of the barn. Since the male suspect has the five-year-old with him in the barn, this is now a hostage situation. Ask for a SWAT team as well."

Brent saw the agent come out slowly from the side of the house, gun raised. With no windows on the front side of the barn, he easily reached Agent Pan without incident.

Pan pressed her earpiece into her ear as one of the agents assigned to the barn began speaking in a low voice. "Team Two, back of the barn, I can see the suspect. He's pacing. The hostage is standing in the middle of the barn."

"Do you see a weapon?" asked Pan.

"One rifle propped up against the stable gate. The horses are getting agitated."

"The gun may be out of his hands now, but he may decide to try to shoot his way out. Back side, can you get a shot?"

"Negative. He's moving around too much, and most of the time the girl's in the way."

"West side, do you have a shot?" she asked.

"That's a negative. Horse stalls on this side of the barn."

"This is east side. Also, negative. Too much equipment in the way. Can't see where hostage is at the moment."

"Damn it," said Agent Pan. "You any good at negotiating, Sergeant Freeman?"

"I'm pretty good."

"Pretty good's better than no good," she said. "You must convince this man, who has nothing to lose, to surrender. No pressure."

Brent and Agent Pan took a position behind a wishing well about five hundred feet from the barn door. His nerves on edge, Brent searched for the words to convince Daryl to give up without hurting Maricella.

"Mr. Townsend," Brent shouted. "This is Sergeant Freeman from the Indianapolis Metropolitan Police Department. I'm here with the FBI. It's over, Mr. Townsend. Send the little girl out and then we can talk about your situation."

Brent waited for an answer. Even though a freezing wind blew, Brent started to sweat. This little five-year-old girl had lost her mother forever and her father to his sins. She had so much life to live. He had to get her out of there.

"Come on, Mr. Townsend," said Brent. "We've already apprehended your accomplices. It's time to give it up. You don't want to hurt her. I heard how you spoke to her when you rode in here."

"Shut up, *Sergeant*," Daryl shouted back. "You know there ain't nothin' to talk about. You and them agents will just come in here and arrest me the minute this kid comes out the door. I'm not going to jail."

"Damn." Pan contacted the agent behind the barn. "Kelly, can you see what's going on in there?"

"He picked up the girl in one arm. Looks like he has a hunting knife in his right hand now. I can't take the shot and guarantee the girl won't get hurt."

"You hear that, Sergeant?" said Pan.

Brent nodded. How could he talk Daryl Townsend into giving up? "What do you want, Mr. Townsend?"

"I want you to get back. I want to see weapons on the ground when me and the girl come out. Otherwise, I'm gonna cut her throat. If I'm goin' down, she's goin' with me."

The cold air stung Brent's lungs as he gasped at the thought. He knew people became desperate when cornered, but he'd never met a man so desperate he'd kill a child to get away.

"He's pulling the horse back out of the stall," said one of the agents. "He put the girl on it and is going to the barn door. I think he's going to try to escape on the horse."

"Where's the knife, Kelly?" asked Pan.

"In a knife holster on his belt. He's behind the horse now, though, and he's picked up the rifle. Still can't get a shot."

Agent Pan looked at Brent. "I have an idea. Everybody listen up." She explained her plan to the others.

"Suspect has unlocked the barn doors and is mounting the horse," said the agent from the back of the barn.

"Stand by." Then after a brief pause Agent Pan shouted, "Now!"

The two agents who came from the sides of the barn flung open the doors, surprising Daryl as the other agents fired their weapons into the ground. The horse reared, threw Daryl and Maricella off his back, and ran towards the woods. Maricella landed on top of Daryl. Brent snatched her up and took her to the side.

As Daryl struggled to breathe, Agent Pan rolled him over and handcuffed him. The two agents from Team Two helped him up and led him out of the barn.

"Who are you?" asked Maricella. "Did God send you?"

"I believe He helped us find you, sweetheart," said Brent.

"Can I go home now?" she asked.

"Soon," he said.

"Maricella, my name is Agent Pan. I want to ask you a quick question."

"Okay."

"You said Jack and Haley are hurt. Do you know where they are?"

"Yeah. They're in a little house in the woods with Chaser."

"Who's Chaser?" asked Brent.

"He's a dog who helped Daryl find us. He's a hunting dog, but he's really nice."

Agent Pan smiled at her and stroked her hair. "Don't worry. We'll find them and make sure to have a doctor take care of them."

"You have to hurry." The poor girl looked frightened. "Daryl shot Jack's leg and hit Haley really hard with his gun."

"It will be okay. We're going to go find them. Right now, I

want you to go with this agent. He's going to take you to the hospital so they can look at you."

"Is my mamá going to be there?"

Brent had been so relieved to find the child he'd nearly forgotten she had no knowledge of her mother's death. "No, not right now. We'll let your family know you're okay and then we'll take you home after the doctor looks at you."

"Okay, but is he a good doctor or a bad one like Dr. Sun?" she asked. "Haley said he was bad because he was going to harvest me." Then she turned back to Brent. "Thank you for saving me."

The shock Brent felt at this innocent statement nearly knocked him over. Did she really know what harvesting meant? Maybe the other children did and that's why they risked escaping in this freezing cold weather. Those two youngsters were the real heroes in this scenario.

"If those kids are hurt as badly as she claims," said Brent, "we need to get on those horses and go find them now. If their injuries don't kill them, the cold might."

Chapter 57

Every time Jack tried to move, a horrible pain shot through his leg. Sometimes it even started to bleed again. He'd had a terrible time keeping Chaser away from it. He'd heard dogs would lick your wounds, but he didn't want Chaser to decide he tasted good. He'd seen Chaser eating the food they hadn't finished the night before. What would Chaser do when all of it disappeared?

Jack heard movement and a groan behind him. "Haley. Haley, can you hear me?"

Her moaning continued. At least he knew she didn't die from the blow of Daryl's gun butt. However, the temperature in the room had dropped significantly since the fire went out. Would anyone come looking for them? Would Lin be angry when Daryl showed up with only one of them? Daryl owned him, but he didn't own Haley.

"Jack?" Haley's voice sounded like a frog croaking.

He turned to see Haley's eyes fluttering. She was regaining consciousness. "I'm here. Try not to move right now. Daryl hit you pretty hard, and he tied us up."

"My head hurts." Haley's face screwed up and she began to cry.

"I know it does. But try not to cry, it might make it worse."

"Where's Mari?"

"He took her with him. He said he couldn't take us all at once. I'm sure he'll be back for you soon. Just try to lie still so you don't hurt yourself more."

"I'm cold."

"Let me see if I can wiggle over next to you so we can keep each other warm." Jack prepared himself for the next round of torture. He had to do it despite the horrendous pain it would cause. If he and Haley didn't stay warm, neither of them would survive.

The minute he started to move, Chaser got up from his sleeping spot and came over. The dog cocked his head at Jack. He got closer and sniffed at Jack's sweaty brow then licked him.

"Stop it, Chaser," Jack shouted through gritted teeth.

Chaser stopped and cocked his head again. He then walked over to Haley and did the strangest thing. He lay down next to her on the opposite side. One more good push and Jack and Chaser would have her sandwiched between them. Maybe Chaser was on their side after all.

"You okay, Jack?"

"I'll be okay. It just hurts if I move too much." Actually, the wound had started bleeding again. It would probably continue to do this off and on until he could get stitches. Of course, he might freeze to death or die from infection if Daryl decided to leave them for good.

Jack could feel Haley's body shaking, not from the cold but from trying not to cry aloud. "Haley, we did the best we could. Maybe there won't be anybody who…you know…for a long time. I bet the cops are still looking for both of you."

"I just feel so bad," she said in a quavering voice. "She's such a sweet little girl. I get it there are kids who need new livers and stuff, but why take one person's life away to help another person?"

"Money. Simple as that. All they care about is making money."

Jack paused, thinking of all the children he'd seen come to the farm in the past five years. No one this young had ever come here since he'd been sold to Daryl. "They never used to do this, so they must have found out they could make lots of money harvesting organs."

"It's sick," declared Haley. "I don't understand. There's lots of ways to make money. They don't have to do this."

"I know, but Haley, I need for you to try to calm down now. We don't want Chaser getting up and leaving you. I suspect you're lots warmer now, aren't you?"

"Yes."

"Close your eyes and try to sleep a little. You're gonna need your rest if I ever figure out how to get loose."

"I'll try," she said.

He could tell she'd started to relax, because the shaking had ceased. Chaser's snore was his second indication. Jack's mind began to whirl as he tried to come up with a solution to their dilemma, but the pain made it hard to think. His leg throbbed from the strain of moving, although the blood had stopped flowing. Maybe a little nap would help. He closed his eyes and nearly drifted off to sleep when he heard voices.

"Haley, wake up. Somebody's here."

Chaser had already awakened to the sounds and stood by the door, tail wagging. Jack nudged Haley. "Haley? Talk to me. Somebody's come to rescue us."

Beginning to panic, Jack yelled. "Help. Help us, please. I think she's dying!"

The door flew open. A man and a woman he'd never seen before entered. The woman's coat had the letters FBI on it. The man knelt down and untied Jack's legs and hands.

"We're the police," he said. "I'm Sergeant Freeman from

Indianapolis and that is Agent Pan from the FBI. What's your name?"

Relieved, the boy began to shake. "Jack, my name is Jack Walters."

"Good to meet you, Jack. I'm going to take a look at your leg and bandage it up to help with any bleeding. We have to take you and Haley out of here by horseback, but there are ambulances waiting for you at the house."

"The house?" said Jack, sitting up. "Did you find Mari? Is she okay?"

"If you mean Maricella, we sure did. You don't have to worry. We've arrested Daryl Townsend, Lin Huang, and Judy Klaussen. Once we've had you checked out at the hospital, we'll contact your family. You can go back to your real home."

"Seriously? I can go home and those people won't be able to hurt any more kids?" asked Jack.

"You can go home, Jack," said the agent. "And those three won't be hurting anyone else."

Jack heard Haley groaning. "Is she okay?"

The FBI agent smiled at him. "She's coming around. We'll get her to the hospital and assess her injuries, but I think she'll be fine."

"I'm okay, Jack," said Haley, then she turned to look at the agent. "Jack's really brave. He tried to save us."

"I know, sweetheart," said Agent Pan. Then she glanced at Jack. "He's the real hero."

Chapter 58

"Well, it looks like none of us had a very merry Christmas this year," said Barnes as she plopped a small package on Brent's desk. "Quit staring at it and open it."

"Since when do we give each other Christmas presents?"

"Open it already."

He shifted his stare from her to the package. He pulled the ribbon and took off the lid. "A key?" he said in confusion. "You already gave me a key."

"We had Christmas dinner with Dad yesterday and I sort of...spilled the beans about your current situation. I told him you'd been staying with us for a while."

"I see."

"Well, he said since he's a bachelor and you're a bachelor, maybe you'd want to stay with him. I think he gets lonely in that big old house by himself." She plopped down in the side chair and propped her elbow on the desk. "It's only temporary until you decide what you want to do. He's got lots of space where you can store your stuff, too. You don't have to do it if you don't want to."

Brent's heart filled with warmth. No matter how bad his relationships were, he could always rely on good friends to have his back. "I think I'll take him up on it. I'm going to take a couple of weeks off, so I won't move in until I return. I promised my mother I'd come home for New Year's Eve since I had to miss

Christmas and...."

"And what? Your mom's okay, isn't she?"

"Yes." He wasn't sure how to tell his former partner and friend about his addiction. As always with Barnes, it would be best to spit it out.

"The day after New Year's I'm going into rehab."

Barnes's mouth dropped open, but it seemed she couldn't find any words to express how she felt about this pronouncement. So he decided he'd explain.

"After I got out of the hospital, I had a hard time sleeping. Natalie got tired of me tossing around in bed and told me to take one of the Vicodin she'd gotten when she had that ankle sprain in August."

Barnes found her voice. "Freeman, the doc told you not to take anything stronger than an Ibuprofen. Was Natalie trying to kill you?"

He ignored her accusation and went on. "I was only going to take them at bedtime, but I kept getting these nasty headaches—a combination of the concussion and all the stress. Anyway, when I realized I'd been taking them so much that I was becoming dependent upon them, I decided I needed help to quit."

"Did you tell Stevenson?"

"I had to tell him. We're so short staffed right now, it's the only way to get that much time off."

"Speaking of attempted murder, have you talked to Natalie at all?"

"No, and I don't see any reason to talk to her," he said. "She's made it very clear she'll never stop this jealousy routine. It's been a nightmare. I should have listened to you and slowed down."

"That's a given."

He noted her smug grin and vowed to make her pay. Maybe he'd assign her the next decomp case when he returned. Movement caught his eye and he saw Detective Samuels escorting Elena Arroyo and Maricella towards him.

"Look who came to visit you, Sergeant Freeman," said Samuels.

"Maricella wanted a chance to thank you, Sergeant," said Elena. "And so do I."

Maricella came up to him and took his hands in hers. "Did you find Jack and Haley?"

"Yes, we did, thanks to you. They're both in the hospital in Louisville, Kentucky where the *good* doctors took care of you. Jack had a pretty bad wound in his leg, so he'll have to stay there for a while. Because Haley had been hit pretty hard on the head, they kept her to do more tests. But her parents are with her now. The doctors say they believe she'll be fine and will be able to go home in a few days."

"Abuela Elena told me Mamá went to Heaven," said Maricella.

"Yes, she did," said Brent.

"Did my papá send her there?"

"Do you remember Nina?"

The child nodded. "Nina helped Daryl take me to his farm. She doesn't like kids."

"She's the one who hurt your mother after your father had asked her to kidnap you. He'd asked Nina to hide you, not to give you to those people on Daryl's farm. He also says he didn't mean for anything to happen to your mother."

Maricella sighed. "He used to say stuff like that all the time. He'd tell Mamá he didn't mean to hurt her, but it was her fault for making him mad. Then he'd say he loved her. It's weird. I think if somebody loves you they shouldn't hit you."

"You are a very smart young lady," said Brent. "You're right. Nobody should do that."

"May I take Maricella to buy her a treat?" asked Samuels.

"Of course," said her grandmother. "You be a good girl and stay with Detective Samuels."

"I will, Abuela."

"Mind if I tag along?" asked Barnes, and the three of them departed.

"I want to thank you for finding my sweet Maricella. She's all I have left."

"We're happy we found her before they could follow through with their plans for her. She's very lucky to have you now that both of her parents are no longer in her life."

"I also want to apologize for how I treated you. I've been a very bitter woman since Javier died. I know you lost two of your detectives while trying to discover who killed him. I'm so sorry, but I do want to thank you for bringing justice to my children. It sickens me to think these people are taking innocent children away from their families every day."

"It sickens all of us, Mrs. Arroyo. Unfortunately, this is so much bigger than anyone could imagine. Thousands of children under seventeen go missing every day. Some run away and become involved in human trafficking, specifically prostitution. However, many are actually grabbed for their looks or ethnicity because someone has put in an order for something specific."

"Los niños pobres. I will not let this child out of my sight. No one will ever hurt my Maricella again."

Chapter 59

Heaviness lay in the middle of Brent's chest this morning. Today Detective Tomas Flores would be laid to rest. His family didn't want to do it until after Christmas; they waited for several of his out of the country family members to arrive.

He'd asked Detective Osaka and a couple of guys from the other two shifts to cover for the day shift today. Of course, they were more than willing to assist. Major Stevenson had announced Osaka would be transferring to the day shift permanently, so he had decided to leave him in charge.

He heard footsteps coming up behind him. It was Samuels and Barnes.

"Get up off your duff. Stevenson wants to see us in the conference room before we leave," said Barnes. Brent rose and she grabbed his arm. "Stop right there. You can't go in looking like that." She took hold of his tie and straightened it, smoothed down his collar, and said, "Better."

When the three of them arrived outside the conference room, Detective Osaka joined them. "Sergeant."

"Osaka, thanks for taking the lead today," said Brent.

"No big deal," said Osaka. "Thanks for trusting me with it. I won't let you down."

Brent grabbed the door handle and led his team inside. Brent felt his jaw drop as he froze in place. Next to Stevenson stood the tall, model-like figure of Chennelle Kendall.

"Well, don't just stand there like gaping fools," said the major. "Have a seat and we'll explain what happened."

Chennelle Kendall looked haggard and ready to cry. Despite her appearance, Brent thought she was the most beautiful thing he'd ever seen.

"I know all of you were led to believe Detective Kendall died after the attack upon her in the hospital," began Major Stevenson. "Since we weren't sure who was behind this and felt Detective Kendall's life was in danger, the FBI and I decided to place Kendall into protective custody to allow the perpetrators to believe she'd died in surgery."

"Did her family know?" asked Samuels.

Major Stevens cleared his throat. "No, they did not. We all know how difficult this decision was on everyone. However, it had to be done to protect her. The fewer people who knew, the less chance someone would divulge our plan."

Brent glanced at Kendall. She looked so unhappy. Chennelle sat there with her head bowed, staring at the table.

"Of course, you must also realize Detective Kendall had no choice. Once the doctors completed the surgery, an ambulance was waiting to take her away. She hadn't come out from under the anesthesia at that point. Believe me; she woke highly protesting the situation."

Kendall's dark cheeks filled with color. Then she ventured a small smile. "He's right. I can't imagine what my family, including all of you, went through this past week. Once they tested the scrapings from my fingernails and discovered Paxton's involvement, they let me come home to my family in time for Christmas dinner."

"I can only imagine their reaction," said Barnes. "If they didn't believe in Christmas miracles before, they do now."

Everyone chuckled and the tension drained from the room. Brent just stared at Chennelle, glad to see her alive and recuperating, but frustrated the major hadn't confided in him. While the other members of the team chattered, welcoming her back, Brent thought he saw tears forming in Barnes's eyes. Then came a knock on the door.

"Major Stevenson, Special Agent Trish Zimmer is on line three," said the clerk. "She said it's urgent."

"Everyone quiet," said the major. He pushed the line button to put the call on speaker. "Agent Zimmer, this is Major Stevenson. I have my team here with me."

"Good, this is something they all should hear."

Zimmer's voice reflected a serious tone that made Brent's hair stand on end. What could have happened now?

"First of all, I want to commend the homicide detectives who were so crucial in this investigation. The sacrifices you've made, both in time and effort and in the loss of police personnel are truly appreciated by the bureau."

"Thank you," said Stevenson.

"However, this call is also about our losses. Late yesterday afternoon, Special Agent Nuwa Pan and four other agents were gunned down at a private airport. They are all deceased." Agent Zimmer paused. "They were in the process of transporting Lin Huang by private jet to Quantico when they were ambushed. We also found airport personnel and our pilot dead. This kept us from discovering the jet hijacking until hours later. I'm afraid Lin Huang has escaped and we're sure she's already out of the country."

Brent had a hard time wrapping his mind around this. Five agents, including Pan, dead. "How do you know she's out of the country?" he asked.

"They had plenty of time to do so. We found our jet in a

remote area northwest of Indianapolis. There were snowmobile tracks, so they'd obviously paid someone to meet them there. The tracks end at Big Springs Road. The closest airport is in Westfield. Personnel there told us a Chinese couple showed up to take their private jet to Chicago."

"Is that where they went?" asked Barnes.

"Yes. We believe they took a commercial flight to San Francisco under false identities. We have some security footage from that airport showing them boarding a flight to Bejing. We didn't discover this until two hours after the plane landed there."

"Do you have any idea who her *husband* was?" asked Major Stevenson.

"From the information we have on this trafficking group, we think the man's name is Zeng Hu. He's Han Wu's bodyguard, pilot, and from what we understand, his hitman. He is likely the person Sergeant Freeman and Agent Pan chased after the Clemente shooting."

"So now what do we do?" asked Brent.

"Nothing unless you have another murder or kidnapping you think is connected. This is big. Bigger than any of us. It's not likely daddy's little girl will be back in the U.S. If he allows her to live, she'll be receiving a big demotion."

"Why would he kill her?" asked Samuels.

"Many Chinese men still don't respect women, even their own daughters. They look at them as expendable. Whether he sent Zeng here to bring her back because she's his daughter or because he thought she might tell us too much remains to be seen."

"Yes, it does," said Kendall.

"Ah, Detective Kendall. It's good to hear your voice," said Zimmer. "I'm so sorry for what we put you and your family through. When you find you're feeling angry with us, just remember, it would have been worse had they been planning a real funeral." Zimmer left a pregnant pause while everyone in the room glanced around at one another.

"I do have more news," said Zimmer. "Judy Klaussen and Daryl Townsend are dead."

Everyone went silent. Then Major Stevenson asked, "How the hell did this happen?"

"The coroner and our lab think its poisoning by some sort of gas." Again, Agent Zimmer waited for her news to sink in.

"Their female attorney insisted on seeing them together. After a few minutes, she asked to go to the restroom and said to keep her clients in the interrogation room and she'd be right back. Surveillance footage shows her, a brunette in a beige coat, entering the restroom on that floor. A few minutes later, a blonde in a black coat emerged, pulled out her cell phone, and left the building."

"How did she administer the gas?" asked Brent.

"They found something similar to a listening device stuck to the bottom of the table in the room. She probably palmed it when she took out some documents from her briefcase and attached it when she used the table to scoot up closer. Forensics are testing it for chemicals as we speak. They believe the woman triggered it with her cell phone."

"A fake cell call by blondie," said Barnes.

"Precisely," said Agent Zimmer. "By the time the guard noticed the suspects had fallen to the floor, the gas had dissipated and the attorney was long gone."

"So now you have no one who can testify about this trafficking ring," said Major Stevenson.

"Unfortunately, that's true. However, we still may locate the Dr. Sun Maricella Colon mentioned. All three children were able to give a pretty good description of him, but it will still take time to locate him. There are thousands of doctors with this last name in the United States. Of course, we can't even be sure he has a practice in this country."

"The proverbial needle in a haystack," said Samuels.

"Major Stevenson, I want to thank you for everything. If I can ever be of service to your department again, don't hesitate to call."

"I'll be in touch, Agent Zimmer," said Stevenson. The phone line went dead as everyone sat in silence. "Unfortunately, we do have a detective who lost his life during this investigation, and we'll be laying him to rest today. Let's go out there and give him the respect and honor he deserves."

Chapter 60

"How's our New England dinner coming, bro?" asked Brenda. "It's going to be ready on time, right?"

Brent grinned at his twin. He found it hilarious that with three sisters, he'd turned out to be the best cook of them all. "This is mom's favorite for New Year's Day, so yes ma'am, it will be ready on time. We can't miss that lucky cabbage, and of course, I'd do anything for my mama."

"Suck up." Brenda grabbed a baby carrot before he could smack her hand away.

"The question is, are Janell, Patty, and their little families going to make it on time."

"Good question." Brenda bit into her carrot, crunched it, and swallowed it before continuing. "I know you had a rough couple of weeks personally, physically, and professionally. How are you doing? Really?"

"Well, Sis, let's start professionally. I can look at it two ways. We caught a big fish who got away, and her father's organization is so big I'm afraid thousands more children will be endangered in the future. Or, I can take my little victory of saving three kids and appreciate it for what it is."

"How are the children?"

"We were able to reunite all of them with their families. Maricella is adorable. I hate the fact her mother's dead and her dad's no good, but she has a wonderful grandmother and aunts to look after her. Haley…" He paused and shook his head. "Haley was amazing. She's one tough little girl. She got out of the hospital yesterday and is back in Indianapolis with her family."

"What happened to the boy?" she asked. "This must be really tough on him."

"This young man has been in captivity for five years. It took a lot for him to defy Daryl and try to rescue Maricella. Jack's healing well from his gunshot wound, but I worry about his mental state. His mother was ecstatic to hear from us, but it's my understanding his father said something like, 'oh, great, another mouth to feed.'"

"Seriously. His son's been missing for five years and that's all he can come up with."

"He's like our dad. He's probably not so much worried about feeding the kid, but about how much more he could be drinking with the money."

"Hopefully, his mother is as wonderful and strong as ours."

"Did I hear something about you having a wonderful mother?"

"Yes, you did, sweetheart," said Brenda. "I hope you know how much we love and appreciate you."

"Suck up," Brent whispered.

His mother came up behind him and gave him a hug. "We'll have this marvelous meal today, and tomorrow Brenda and I will take you to the hospital."

"Thanks, Mom," he said. He'd continued to take the Vicodin, but under a doctor's care this time since he'd passed the danger point. The doctor had given him a limited number of pills with the understanding he would be going into rehab the day after New Year's.

"Brent, your cell phone keeps ringing." She paused, frowning and pursing her lips. "I'm sure it's Natalie. She's the one who kicked you out. I don't understand why she keeps calling."

"Sorry, Mom. I'll call her back right now and tell her to stop calling." He set down his chopping knife and walked towards the den. Mom and Brenda would be whispering about this the minute he closed the door. What did Natalie want? Mom was right; Natalie threw him out, and she hadn't called him for nearly two weeks, but all of a sudden, she wanted to talk.

Brent picked up the cell phone, bracing himself for the worst. He speed dialed her number and she picked up right away.

"Are you in Kokomo?"

Although none of her business, Brent decided to answer her. "Yes. I missed Christmas because of a case and promised Mom I'd come for New Year's." He'd said too much. Why did he always think he needed to explain himself?

"I thought we'd be spending New Year's Eve together."

Brent's head began to spin. Was *she* on something? How could she possibly think after all she'd said they'd be going out for New Year's Eve? "Really?"

"Yes. You promised we'd go downtown this year and stay at the Hilton."

"Natalie, that was before you packed all my stuff in boxes and told me to go somewhere else to sleep."

"I thought once you'd had time to think about it, you'd see your error and would come back. You know you love me and I love you. We belong together."

Brent's temper rose until he thought his head would burst, increasing his desire for another Vicodin. "No, Natalie, we don't belong together. Loving each other isn't enough. I can't live with someone who watches my every move."

"So, did you take pretty Agent Pan to meet your mother this

weekend?"

Now she'd gone too far. "Even if I did, it's none of your business anymore." His voice was increasing in volume with every word. "But for your information, Agent Pan, along with several other agents, were killed in the line of duty. This bull is exactly why I'm not coming back."

Silence. Brent stood there, his chest heaving, tempted to throw his phone across the room. He wanted to hurt her for her lack of sensitivity. The news had reported Pan's death for the last couple of days and he knew it had to be all over the office by now. He questioned Natalie's mental state.

She finally broke the silence. "Well, then. Is it okay for me to come to Kokomo?"

Aghast, Brent shouted at her. "No! You and I are through."

"You don't mean that," she said. Her voice cracked.

"I do mean it. I don't want to be cruel, but you need to lose my number. From now on, we are professional colleagues and that's it."

"There's someone else, isn't there?" She now sounded calm, scary calm.

"No."

"Whoever she is, she isn't good enough for you. I'm not giving up. If I can't have you, no one else can."

The line went dead. This time Brent did throw his phone. In moments, his sister and mother rushed into the room.

Brenda picked up his phone, showing him the spider web crack in his screen. "She must have really ticked you off this time."

He realized he'd just broken off all communication with the police department, something he could not do and keep his job. As soon as he calmed down, he'd ask to use Brenda's phone to call in with his mother's home number, since he couldn't get a new phone today.

"Mom, can you finish cutting up the veggies?" he asked. "I need to get myself together. Wielding a lethal weapon isn't a very good idea right now."

"Of course, I can, dear."

"Brenda, would you take me for a drive? I'm too ticked to drive right now, but I really need some fresh air."

He and Brenda grabbed their coats and got into her car. Brent shook, resisting the urge to go back inside for one of his pills. He knew Brenda wanted an explanation, and he wanted to give her one as soon as he calmed down.

"Spew, bro," she said. "You may as well get it all out now so you can tell it to Mom without shouting at her."

"That woman...she...I don't believe her." He proceeded to give her a blow-by-blow version of the conversation.

"Brent, she sounds like one of those crazy stalkers."

"I'm sure when she has time to think about it, she'll see I'm right and move on. The sooner, the better."

"You know, I'm sure all those people I watch on those real crime TV programs thought the same thing. Almost all of them thought the person wouldn't harm them, and now they're dead. Please be careful."

He could see genuine concern in his twin's eyes, so he tried to make light of it. "Well, if she does kill me, I have a top-notch homicide team to solve it."

"Not funny. I mean it. She's losing it. At the very least, make sure you tell Major Stevenson and Erica. I know they'll look out for you. Plus, you need to get a restraining order."

"Okay, okay. If it will make you feel better I'll talk to them as soon as I get back." He loved the fact his twin wanted to protect him. Despite his bravado, Natalie had scared him. A restraining order would be a good idea. Hopefully, his absence would give her time to cool off and come to her senses. Never again would he jump into a relationship so quickly. Never.

ABOUT THE AUTHOR

Michele May, whose pen name is M. E. May, was born in Indianapolis, Indiana, and lived in central Indiana until she met her husband and moved to the suburbs of Chicago Illinois, in 2003. Although, she has physically moved away, her heart still resides in her hometown. She has a son, a daughter, and four grandsons still living in central Indiana.

Michele studied Social and Behavioral Sciences at Indiana University, where she learned how the mind and social circumstances influence behavior. While at the university, she also discovered her talent for writing. Her interest in the psychology of humans sparked the curiosity to ask why they commit such heinous acts upon one another. Other interests in such areas as criminology and forensics have moved her to put her vast imagination to work writing fiction that is as factual as possible.

Michele is an active member of Mystery Writers of America Midwest Chapter, Sisters in Crime Chicagoland, Speed City Sisters in Crime in Indianapolis, and the Chicago Writers Association.

Her *Circle City Mystery Series* is appropriately named as these stories take place in her home town of Indianapolis. The first novel in the series, *Perfidy*, won the 2013 Lovey Award for Best First Novel in Chicago.